Praise for Bonnie Dee & Summer Devon's *The Gentleman's Keeper*

"Devon and Dee fill this expertly written gay Victorian romance with emotional tension...this deep story is a must-read for fans of gay historicals."

~ *Publishers Weekly*

"...what I loved the most was the burning tension between the characters from the moment they meet."

~ *Dear Author*

"...one of the best historical romances I have read this year. The story has a rare richness and depth, and its many layers are lovingly revealed by these two talented authors."

~ *Night Owl Reviews*

"*The Gentleman's Keeper* is another sweet and enjoyable historical romance from Bonnie Dee and Summer Devon. Seeing their names on a book pretty much guarantees I'm going to like the contents."

~ *Joyfully Reviewed*

"I was brought into the world the authors created and felt captivated from the first page all the way to the last."

~ *Gaylist Book Reviews*

Look for these titles by
Bonnie Dee

Now Available:

Finding Home *(with Lauren Baker)*
Evolving Man
Blackberry Pie
Opposites Attract
Perfecting Amanda
The Valentine Effect
The Countess Takes a Lover
The Final Act
Empath
The Countess Lends a Hand
Butterfly Unpinned *(with Laura Bacchi)*
The Thief and the Desert Flower
Star Flyer
The Au Pair Affair

Magical Menages
Shifters' Captive
Vampires' Consort

Writing with Summer Devon
The Psychic and the Sleuth
Fugitive Heart
The Gentleman's Keeper
The Gentleman's Madness

Fairytale Fantasies
(with Marie Treanor)
Cinderella Unmasked
Demon Lover
Awakening Beauty
Sex and the Single Princess

Print Anthologies
Heat Wave
Strangers in the Night
Gifted

Look for these titles by
Summer Devon

Now Available:

Learning Charity
Revealing Skills
Knight's Challenge
Taken Unaware
Unnatural Calamities
Taming the Bander
Sibling Rivals

Writing with Bonnie Dee
The Psychic and the Sleuth
Fugitive Heart
The Gentleman's Keeper
The Gentleman's Madness

Print Anthology
I Dream of Dragons, Volume 1

The Gentleman's Keeper

Bonnie Dee & Summer Devon

SAMHAIN
PUBLISHING

Samhain Publishing, Ltd.
11821 Mason Montgomery Road, 4B
Cincinnati, OH 45249
www.samhainpublishing.com

The Gentleman's Keeper
Copyright © 2014 by Bonnie Dee & Summer Devon
Print ISBN: 978-1-61921-934-2
Digital ISBN: 978-1-61921-726-3

Editing by Linda Ingmanson
Cover by Lou Harper

First Samhain Publishing, Ltd. electronic publication: July 2013
First Samhain Publishing, Ltd. print publication: July 2014

Dedication

To the Ipsials we've known, and to Linda for the adverbs.

Prologue

Horses frightened him, so he rode as often as possible. Great heights made him dizzy and nauseated, so he climbed to the top of every church tower he could. He loathed violence but got into more scrapes than any other boy of his year. Both of Everett Gerard's names meant brave and strong, and, by God, he'd live up to the names, no matter what his mewling inner self desired.

His first task at school was to shed the nickname bestowed upon him within an hour of his arrival by his awful cousin, Hubert. Losing the name of "Eve" proved easy enough to accomplish—he took on anyone who called him that.

Small of stature and not particularly strong, Gerard rarely won fights, but he also never quit the battlefield. He became quite familiar with the school's sick room, and he suffered two broken noses and a broken arm before he went to university.

By the time he reached his twenty-fifth year, he'd grown nearly tall and strong enough to suit his own specifications, and perhaps even his father's requirements for a Gerard, though he'd never know, for the *pater familias* suddenly died.

The moment Gerard heard of his father's death, he stopped the fight.

His father's approval, if such a thing existed, would remain unexpressed for all time. The other reason the younger Gerard had engaged in combat also seemed doomed to failure. He could not root out certain undesirable portions of his nature.

He hadn't lost all his internal battles. When it came to his cringing secret self, he'd overcome most of his long list of fears and only one remained. Although could his distaste for his family's country home, the abbey, be called fear? At any rate, Gerard had no interest in conquering that particular dread, so he simply stayed away. After his father's death, he lived in London except for an excursion to Italy.

He ignored correspondence from the abbey as well, until one morning in September when he no longer could.

Chapter One

London 1888

"Sir? You must read this one." Farley, his valet/secretary, dropped something light on Gerard's chest.

Gerard roused from an uncomfortable doze. He blinked and looked down at himself, or rather up. Dressed in rumpled eveningwear, he appeared to have his boots on, and yes, his feet were propped on a chair. He lay on his back on the hearthrug next to the drawing room fireplace. He clutched a wilted glove in one hand. In the other he held an almost empty brandy glass. A white object lay on his chest—the piece of paper and an envelope Farley had dumped on him.

"What time is it?" His voice came out as a croak. His head hurt, but he'd felt worse in the last year of dissipation.

"Ten a.m., sir." With a long sigh, the portly Farley sank onto the chair near the fireplace. Gerard turned his head enough to see that the valet had also polished his own boots to a perfect shine.

"That early, eh? Wonder what time I got back."

"Sir arrived home four hours ago and refused to go to bed." Farley's words dripped with disdain.

"That I recall." Gerard touched his aching head, and the paper on his chest rustled. "What the devil did you drop on me just now?"

"A letter from the abbey's gamekeeper, sir."

"Pickens?" Hadn't he died years, more than a decade,

earlier? Gerard had a vague memory of a man with a squint and a tray of cheeping baby birds.

"No, sir. Mr. Kenway is now our gamekeeper."

Gerard remembered the interview, as he'd been quite knackered from an evening's festivities. Mr. Miles Kenway from Yorkshire by way of Canada, or perhaps the other way around. He had a peculiar accent, mostly the long, soft vowels of Yorkshire. And he had shoulders that barely fit through the doorway of the solicitor's office.

"He's a bailiff, or steward. Not gamekeeper. No one has hunted at the abbey for years. I recall Kenway. He's that hulking man I hired a while back. The one with the voice sounded like the toll of a church's funeral bell."

"Very poetic, sir. Kenway claims he has sent us two letters already."

"You opened my mail?"

"Yes, sir. Surely he is mistaken, sir? *Two* previous letters?" When Farley spoke in first person plural and added many sirs to his speech, he was more annoyed than usual. He rose to his feet. A servant must not sit in his master's presence, and on occasion Farley remembered he was Gerard's servant.

"I doubt he's lying." Gerard had tossed several letters into the fire, telling himself he needed the space on his desk.

Throwing away unwanted correspondence—when had he turned into such a coward? He patted his chest until he found the paper.

Farley loomed over him, waiting.

"Yes, I was wrong to toss the letters away. Stop the sniffing noises, Farley. See? I pick up the paper like so, unfold and read it... The man has the most appalling hand, and...eh? What?" He squinted and read again. "What in God's name does Kenway mean 'my son'? I have no son."

"Are you certain of that, sir?"

"Yes." Gerard didn't elaborate.

Farley made a soft, disbelieving grunt. He was convinced Gerard's recent habit of dissipation included bedding women. Gerard had once overheard the valet telling a footman that he should be ashamed to believe the rumors; a manly man like Mr. Gerard would never have spent the night in the Conte Azzari's bed.

Farley was technically correct. Gerard and the count had only been in the bed for four hours, hardly the whole night. There'd been an invigorating hour on the floor as well.

A month before breaking a lifetime's fast with Azzari, Gerard had received the news of his father's death. At that news, all virtue, self-discipline and temperance had flown out the window like a flock of doves—and no birds had flown back to the roost since.

Gerard pulled his feet off the chair and sat up, groaning softly. He held up the letter to read one more time. "Oh, well, of course it can't be. This so-called son of mine is about nine years old, so I would have been in school when he was conceived."

"Yes, sir." Farley leaned over and plucked the letter from his hand. He held something in his other hand, a tintype.

Gerard took it from him. A thin, unhappy face peered at the world. The heavy Gerard eyes and the distinctive full lower lip. Christ. He looked down at a copy of his own features and attitude in a much younger face.

"Well. Whoever his father might be, he's certainly one of us," Gerard said.

He pulled the letter away from Farley, who was reading it again. He'd probably memorized the good bits, of which there were plenty.

Kenway had written: *The boy arrived here by foot, half starved. His mother gave him your name and direction, a train ticket and information about your family, but little else, not even proper shoes. The servants are convinced he is your child.*

The man's indignation showed in every scrawled line. Apparently Miles Kenway didn't care if he offended his employer. He didn't hint or approach the subject crabwise or skirt around it.

You must come to the abbey. No one else has the authority to cope with the situation. I had thought a simple letter of instruction from you might be enough, but I am afraid we require you here as soon as possible.

He had some cheek, Garret thought without anger. Perhaps he would interview other possible bailiffs, because this one apparently didn't want to keep the job.

"I'm warning you, put it down. Now. And carefully. Don't aim it at me or the windows." Miles was fairly sure he'd unloaded the shotgun, but who knew? Maybe the young devil knew how to load guns.

"Why should I?"

Miles examined the scarecrow-thin figure who seemed too scrawny to lift the weapon. "If you do, I'll teach you to shoot properly. If you don't, you'll end up learning about birdshot too well, my boy."

No. *Not* his boy, thank God. Though unfortunately the young devil was more his than anyone else's. If any abbey servant should want to find young Ipsial Gerard, they'd ask Miles. If they did ask, usually they wanted to be able to stay away from the troublesome lad.

Standing in the middle of the room, the boy narrowed his heavy-lidded eyes at Miles. "You'll teach me to shoot?" There was pure disbelief in the voice.

"Yes, I promise." They'd had similar conversations before. Miles would make a promise and then listen to Ipsial's scoffing disbelief. No matter that so far Miles had kept the promises. The boy never believed the next one.

Ipsial had grown better in the weeks he'd been at the abbey, Miles supposed. He no longer cursed as much. He'd stopped trying to steal wallets—mostly. He actually engaged in conversation rather than trying to escape Miles's house with food tucked under his hideous jacket. And the boy stole only a meal's worth now, instead of as much as he could carry.

When Miles had arranged the picture-taking with a traveling photographer, the boy had protested for only half an hour and hadn't attempted to invade the man's wagon or annoy his horse. That counted as progress.

Ipsial sniffed. He touched the gun's stock, peered into the barrels, the young idiot. He looked around the main room of Miles's cottage with feigned interest.

Miles counted to ten slowly. He could wait out animals, and this boy was certainly a beast. After what had to be two full minutes of pretending to think about it, Ipsial lowered Miles's gun and put it on the rough wooden plank floor.

He watched Miles, smirking. The big pale blue eyes dared him to protest at how slow he'd been to obey, but Miles stayed silent and allowed him the victory. Miles usually did when it came to the details. Let the fiend win in small matters.

Ipsial. Miles tried to think of him using the silly name no one else would. The name wasn't from the Old Testament as the staff had first guessed. Joey, who acted as groundsman, footman and groom all rolled into one, had quipped, *"Unless Satan wrote a version of the Bible?"*

Certainly everyone else on the estate called him the young devil.

Everyone agreed Ipsial had made a nest somewhere on the estate. Miles suspected it was the hut that had once belonged to the abbey's gardener, but he didn't go inside to make sure. Wild animals tended to abandon their homes if humans poked around too much.

Miles went to the shotgun and cracked it open. Loaded and ready to fire.

"Christ." He rarely cursed.

"What?" Ipsial slunk to the door. "I put it down," he whined.

"So you did. Tomorrow morning, an hour's lesson." Miles held back a sigh. The boy fled the cottage without a backward look.

Miles sat down heavily on the only chair in the room. The door still stood ajar, and a stiff breeze pushed through the crack. Would Ipsial try to light a fire to stay warm? He hadn't burned down a house yet.

Miles laughed. He'd been a fool to think he missed the sound of childish voices when he'd first arrived at the estate. He'd thought he liked children, and so he did—most children. He had no illusions about childish innocence or pure souls. They could be cruel with one another as any man in war. Still, he liked their shrieks and their play, and he even enjoyed the endless questions his nephew and niece plagued him with.

Ipsial, though he said he was nine or perhaps ten, was like no child Miles had met, except perhaps the abandoned orphan he'd seen in Halifax. That boy had been on trial for murdering his grandparents.

16

Miles had come back to his cottage for a midday meal, but finding Ipsial there with the gun had stirred his ire, again. Now he grabbed a chunk of two-day-old bread and gnawed it as he strode through the edge of the woods, past the overgrown gardens, over the surprisingly tidy lawns to the servants' entrance of the abbey.

Mrs. Billings, the housekeeper, was alone in the servants' dining hall, eating some sort of stew. She rose at once, graceful for such a large lady. No doubt the state of the lawns was due to her influence. He wondered if she scared the day gardeners as much as she frightened her own staff.

She kept her black dress and black hair in starched, spotless perfection, and the lace at her sleeves and neck remained pure white. Never mind that the master of the house had been absent during her entire tenure. As she was fond of telling people, Mrs. Billings had recently worked in the household of an earl and kept the standards high in any position she held.

She folded her hands in front of her and eyed Miles as if he was a workman and not the steward. "If you have any game, leave it in the kitchen. Are your boots muddy?"

"No game, and my boots are fine." Worn down, certainly, but he kept them clean. "I want to know if Gerard has been in contact with any of you lot."

"*Mr.* Gerard has not."

He paced the room. "Has he always been such an unreliable sod?"

"I fail to understand that word," she said with a sniff.

If he didn't apologize at once, she'd read him a lecture as if he was a slovenly parlor maid, and he'd never get an answer. "Beg pardon. I should say, has Mr. Gerard always been so irresponsible in his duties?"

"We do *not* gossip in this hall and—"

He interrupted before she could get a full head of steam. "I ask because of the boy."

"Ah." She sat at the table again. "You have been in contact with the lawyer, Mr. Chambers, I understand?"

"That was a month past, and he promised to contact Gerard immediately. I've heard nothing. You'd think a solicitor would give a da—would care that his client suddenly gained an heir. Or maybe the master's ignoring him as well."

She picked up her spoon and ate a small mouthful of stew before answering. "The members of staff I hired from the valley and village have stories of Mr. Gerard's late father, a stern but fair man."

A bastard, Joey the catch-all servant had said.

"But none knows the younger Mr. Gerard. There are rumors from London, though of course one doesn't believe everything one hears."

A few months earlier, a London friend had laughed when Miles told him the name of his employer. *"Keep your references handy, Kenway. I've heard Gerard plans to drink himself to death before thirty."* The friend had promised to keep his eyes open for something steadier for Miles, but they both knew times were difficult. Miles, restless though he was, could ill afford to leave a good job.

Miles walked over to the fireplace. He picked up a poker and shoved a stray coal back into the glowing heart of the fire. He said, "I've heard one or two stories of the man."

Mrs. Billings wrinkled her long nose. "Bah, someone's cousin's servant claims Mr. Gerard is a libertine. I hold no stock in such nonsense."

The translation of her statement was simple: she couldn't

bear to be in charge of a household run by a less than respectable gentleman.

Miles kept his mouth shut, though he disagreed. Even if he hadn't talked to his London friend, Miles would be inclined to believe the rumor of Gerard as a wild man. Made sense Ipsial's sire would be as rackety in the head as the boy.

"I'm sorry I cannot help you. Do you require anything further, Mr. Kenway?"

He carefully replaced the poker. "No, thank you, Mrs. Billings." A bit late now to act the part of polite servant—if only he'd measured his words before sending those letters. He needed this job. Those letters he'd written Gerard would annoy the mildest of employers.

A pity he'd lost his temper when his sister depended on the money he sent her.

Could he manage an apology? No, for he remained thoroughly disgusted by the lad's father. If he was going to act against his inclinations, he'd contact his London friend and others—everyone he knew—to beg them for help to find new work. And between writing those groveling letters, he'd do what he could with Ipsial. He doubted anyone else would take on the drunkard's spawn; obviously not the drunkard himself. Before Miles moved along, he'd do his best to tame the boy.

Chapter Two

They passed the ugly coal mining towns, past the darkened, cramped cottages of the miners and then the town with steel workers, back to fields and a smaller village where farms still ruled the landscape. The closer the carriage got to the abbey, the rougher the roads were—and the more Gerard's leg jiggled. He couldn't seem to stop the restless movement of his body or the growing anxiety that made his chest ache and his breathing erratic. A particularly painful lurch of the carriage as it bumped over a washed-out road made his teeth click together, nipping the end of his tongue. The sudden sharp pain brought tears to his eyes—or maybe they were from the sight of the horrid, desolate moor that he'd sworn never to clap eyes on again. He'd fled the country and his childhood home for good reason. Only an unexpected miracle could have dragged him back.

Although, could the immaculate conception that produced an heir be considered a miracle? More like a curse. No doubt the curse carried the name Cousin Hubert. Good luck to any lad who tried to claim Halfwit Hubie as father.

Gerard had fully intended to let his family line die with himself, and even now he didn't care if the house crumbled, a haunted ruin around which ravens circled. But suddenly, all because of a boy who happened to have features similar to his own, he was facing the mossy stone wall that surrounded the grounds and driving the familiar path toward the forbidding monstrosity that would alarm any sane person. Despite himself, Gerard leaned forward and pressed his cheek against the window to get a better view of the house.

The gardens were somewhat overgrown but better maintained than he'd expected. And the rambling building, which had once housed an order of monks, looked little like the Gothic gargoyle he'd painted in his mind.

See what happens when one faces one's fears? Just a house after all.

The thought was barely formed when something hit the side of the carriage, not the thump of a small animal crushed beneath the great iron wheels, but a rattling as if someone had fired scattershot at the vehicle. Gerard jerked away from the door, and Farley woke with a snort and bolted upright. "What?"

Although a web of cracks marked the window, no pellets had pierced the siding. Gerard leaned close to the window to peer around, searching for the perpetrator of the attack. He thought he saw a figure disappear behind one of the hedges.

The carriage halted, and Farley muttered sleepily, "Are we there?"

The driver jumped down from the box and opened the door. "Are you all right, sir? Some ragged urchin hurled a slingshot full of stones at the vehicle, then ran away."

A child. Just a child. Not some vengeful spirit from his past come to warn him away from the place. "I'm fine," Gerard assured the man. "Although the window's the worse for wear. Drive on."

The door closed, and the driver resumed his seat and chirruped to the horses.

"A stone-throwing urchin?" The valet shifted his bulk and straightened his immaculate, if rumpled, waistcoat. "Are there many such in the country? Perhaps it was the child of a staff member. If so, then someone must be called to task for letting their progeny run loose about the estate."

Gerard mulled over the idea. "I've a strong suspicion that the lad may be the reason for our visit—my supposed long-lost heir."

Farley fell silent, checking the time on his pocket watch as he often did when nonplussed. "Someone should take charge of the boy, sir, and not allow him to run wild."

"Who? There's no nanny or governess in residence. Whose responsibility is he, do you suppose? It's not the housekeeper's place to control the lad's behavior."

Farley slipped the lid of the watch closed with a firm click. "The sooner the issue of the child's paternity is resolved, the better, sir. Your solicitor should be able to track down something about his mother's history and uncover the truth. In the meantime, you might hire some local woman to care for the boy until you ship him off to either an orphanage or boarding school."

Farley's bossy familiarity was becoming tiring. "Yes. I am well aware of what needs to be done, thank you."

Gerard turned his attention back to the window in time to glimpse the sundial that had always stood in the part of the garden nearest the front door. It looked exactly the same as he remembered from his boyhood. Close up, he supposed the stone would be more weathered, but how odd that while he'd lived so many years away from this place, the sundial had stood there in all seasons, unchanging. There seemed something profound about that.

The carriage rolled to a stop. Gerard didn't wait for the driver but flung open the door and jumped down onto the gravel drive. He faced the front door of the house that had sheltered Gerards since King Henry had rousted the Catholics. The sprawling stone abbey was a piece of history plunked down in the north country. He tried to feel some connection with his deceased ancestors but felt only dread at the prospect of entering those thick doors.

Before he could whip up his courage to mount the steps and use the knocker to summon the staff, the door opened and a woman in a crisp white apron emerged.

"Mr. Gerard." She greeted him with a curtsy. "I'm Mrs. Billings. It's good to make your acquaintance, sir. I hope you'll find everything in order."

Mrs. Billings the housekeeper. Of course. Gerard dipped his head. "Pleased to meet you. I'm sure you've kept the place in fine shape."

A flurry of activity followed as Mrs. Billings ushered him into the front hall and a single manservant went to gather the travelers' boxes, trunks and bundles. Farley oversaw the transport of luggage while Gerard looked around at the age-darkened paintings and the Gerard coat of arms mounted on one wall. The walls were stone and the hall was as cold and dim as a crypt, even with its line of high, arched windows.

As Mrs. Billings led him farther into the newer wing, Gerard realized the place wasn't nearly as large or impressive as he'd thought when he was a child. In fact, it was quite shabby although spotlessly clean.

"I've put you in the blue room, as the furniture in the main suite is quite musty from age and the mattress lumpy. I'm sorry, but I thought you'd prefer the more modernized and comfortable room," Mrs. Billings apologized as they walked up the wide staircase to the first story.

"You thought correctly, Mrs. Billings." His dead father's room was the last place he wanted to sleep, even if the old man had rarely been here to use it.

He might as well get the worst over with. Without meeting her eye, he asked, "I wondered if you could tell me more about young Ipsial. Where is the lad?"

She inhaled sharply but answered without hesitation. "That I couldn't tell you, sir. He runs about the place quite uncontrollably. I'm sorry, but I was uncertain how you wanted me to proceed, whether I should hire a caretaker for him, and so I'm afraid he's been allowed to remain quite...wild."

An odd choice of words. Gerard recalled the smattering of stones and the running figure. His sense of dread over being back in his boyhood home was eclipsed by a different dread about meeting this apparently uncivilized child. What was he supposed to do with it? He'd never even kept a pet, for God's sake.

Mrs. Billings opened the bedroom door and stepped back for him to enter. The room had quite a modern décor and fresh appearance. Apparently his father had at some point attempted to bring the abbey up to snuff but abandoned the project midway. Pouring money into a house no one wanted to live in was, after all, a fruitless task.

"After you've refreshed yourself from your journey I could bring tea to the study, if you care to partake, sir." Mrs. Billings bustled around with an efficiency that rivaled Farley's, twitching the corner of the bedcover back into place, adjusting the curtain so it hung just so.

"Thank you, Mrs. Billings." He dismissed her and exhaled in relief when the energetic housekeeper vacated the room.

Gerard moved to stand at the window and observe the grounds below. No wild child lurked in the gardens, but a figure was striding swiftly from the distant woods toward the manor house, a tall, broad-shouldered, rather hulking figure. Ah, that would be the bailiff, the one who wrote admonishing letters to his employer.

Gerard remembered the perfunctory interview he'd had

with the man and the impression he'd gotten of utter forthrightness and capability. He'd hired Miles Kenway in London and sent him to manage the estate he refused to attend to himself. If Kenway had thought it odd his new employer didn't meet him at the property to show him around, he didn't display any curiosity. Perhaps he'd simply been grateful to gain employment when his own work history had so many halts and starts in it. The man apparently moved every few years and not simply from job to job. He traveled at least a hundred miles with each new position. Gerard recalled now that he'd explained it as restlessness, a streak of gypsy blood? No, he looked entirely English.

Annoyance and a strange anticipation mingled in him as he watched the looming figure draw closer. There was no doubt Kenway had seen his arrival and was coming to address him on the subject of his supposed progeny. Why did Gerard feel like a schoolboy about to be reprimanded by the headmaster, and why did a ridiculous fillip of something like eagerness make his heart beat faster? It wasn't the prospect of making decisions about the child but had more to do with something about the powerful presence of the bailiff.

Too long with nothing intriguing in his life, he decided. Gambling and racing, boxing and dancing, sexual dalliances and alcohol—he'd indulged in every vice and amusement possible for a wealthy man. He'd cut a swath across Europe and ended the journey sated yet unfulfilled. At least this journey to his roots promised something different. Discomfort, perhaps.

Gerard quickly washed and changed after Farley arrived with the bags. He waved away his valet's attempts to give a last shine to his shoes and hurried down to the parlor.

Miles Kenway already awaited him there, cap in hands, big muddy boots threatening to give Mrs. Billings conniptions as they tracked the carpet.

25

"Mr. Everett." Kenway greeted him with a bow. "I'm glad you've come."

The Yorkshire lilt coupled with something imported from Canada was easy on the ears. Gerard nearly smiled but recalled why he was there and kept his expression neutral.

"I understand I've become a father. Now, tell me all about the boy." He gestured to one of the chairs. "Take a seat."

He watched the large man fold himself and perch on the edge of a ridiculously fragile-looking chair. Apparently the receiving room was one of Father's remodeling projects. When had the old man packed away the massive, dark pieces that used to dominate this room?

He looks like a mastiff perched on a lap dog's cushion. Gerard suppressed his natural exuberance and maintained the gravity suitable for such an occasion. But, oh, the man's forbidding countenance, the nose that had obviously been broken at least once, the rough-hewn features, made him want to tease. What would Kenway be like if stirred to anger? A glorious and frightening sight to behold, Gerard had no doubt. A sight he'd like to see.

Miles had met Mr. Gerard only the one time, in Gerard's London solicitor's office for his employment interview. He hadn't had much time to develop an opinion of his new employer, but he was good at reading men's characters, and he'd seen Gerard as a dissolute bounder with too much money and too little common sense.

In the intervening time, Gerard had confirmed his opinion by repeatedly acting blasé about Miles's quarterly reports or his requests for changes to be made to the estate.

Do whatever you think needs to be done, Gerard had airily responded in one of his rare personal correspondences—usually they only communicated through the solicitor. *That's why I hired you, so I don't have to think about it.*

And so Miles had trudged on, doing his duty to the best of his ability. He'd come to care for the land and its tenants. He was, to all intents and purposes, the lord of the manor, making all the decisions that Gerard should have been making. Worse still, the landowner's father had directed the local solicitor to give only the barest minimum to running the house and its immediate environs. Despite Kenway's pleas and the begging of the man who held the job before him, the son seemed just as much of a skinflint as the father, and even less responsive—until today.

Gadabout Gerard, Miles had begun referring to the man in his mind. But now that he faced the man in the flesh, he was struck by something unexpected in the man's eyes. While amusement sparkled on the cool blue surface, beneath it he sensed something dark and deep, a profound sense of loss or pain or sadness. He wasn't certain which. Maybe all three. Maybe none of them. It could simply be the heavy-lidded eyes that suggested a sorrow or depth that wasn't there.

"As I said in my letters," Miles began, feeling strongly that Gerard had barely skimmed what he'd written if he'd read them at all, "Ipsial showed up more than a month ago with a note in hand claiming his paternity, and a carpet bag with a few clothes and possessions over one shoulder. Not knowing whether he was truly related or not, we—meaning the staff, sir—decided to put him in the guests' cottage rather than a guest room. We couldn't be sure he wouldn't run off with the silver or anything else he got his hands on if allowed indoors."

"Mrs. Billings called the lad 'wild'." Gerard had poured a pair of glasses of brandy and now offered one to Miles before sitting across from him. "What did she mean by that?"

"Exactly as it sounds, sir. The boy has apparently spent much of his life fending for himself. He abandoned that cottage but remains on the premises. I believe he's picked another outlying building that hasn't been used for years."

Gerard narrowed his eyes at this but didn't speak, so Miles continued, "He steals food on a regular basis and gets into anything he can possibly get into. He's uncivilized, probably unlettered, and some days I doubt whether he's even human."

Remembering who he was talking to, Miles dipped his head. "Sorry, sir. The little hellion *is* improving, I believe. I've been treating him as I would a horse that's been abused, and I think he's slowly coming to trust that no one here means him any harm."

"But he's clearly not ready for boarding school, although, God knows, the place is full of nasty little animals." Gerard tapped a finger against his glass. "I can't take him home with me, and it would be quite wrong of me to leave him clattering around here with some poor, hapless governess to look after him."

"In my opinion, he's in need of more than lessons. He needs someone to watch him full time, but he's too old for a nanny," Miles said, hoping that Gadabout would see the seriousness of the situation. "If handled with care, I believe Ipsial could grow into a responsible, civilized human being."

"It sounds as if you've grown fond of the boy." Gerard studied him with intent blue eyes that made Miles shift uncomfortably in his chair. Perhaps Gadabout wasn't as oblivious as he seemed.

"I believe there's good in him and that it can be cultivated," Miles said simply.

The other man nodded and set down his empty glass. "I suppose I should meet the boy. My...son, if the stories he tells are to be believed. I have my London solicitor looking into that."

"We can walk the grounds and try and roust the boy, but if he doesn't wish to be found, we shan't see him today. At any rate, this will give me an opportunity to tour the land with you and give you a report."

"I don't believe I need a tour." There was more than a touch of asperity in his voice. "I assume the tenants are content?"

Miles suppressed a sigh. "Yes, the funds to repair the rental properties are just adequate, and the farm is productive." Unfortunately, the solicitor kept a close eye on those funds, or Miles would have shifted some pounds to use on the abbey roof. "The several cottages owned by your family are among the most sought after in the village. But the abbey and its outbuildings are—"

"The servants are paid?"

"Yes, although, as you instructed, the last of the gardeners was let go. Only one man remains, and he's only here four days a week." Miles didn't bother to hold back his rising temper. "Sir, there is a matter of upkeep and repairs to your family's home."

Miles ignored Gerard's grunt of annoyance and continued, "I have the skill required to do most of the repairs necessary, and I do not mind such work. For the other necessary repairs, I can find a farmer willing to work instead of pay rent."

"No."

Again, Miles ignored Gerard, though his employer's eyes had narrowed and his full mouth gone tight.

"As I've mentioned in the letter I sent, sir"—to be entirely accurate three of the letters he'd sent—"the only holdup is that the purchase of materials for the abbey's preservation. Mortar is crumbling. There are at least two cottages within the grounds that require more than rethatching. The repair I have done on the abbey roof is temporary, and I will need better materials to replace the whole of the east-wing roof."

"Are you deaf, Kenway? No."

Miles clamped his teeth tight but managed to get out the words. "Then, sir, the buildings, the abbey itself will fall to ruins within two generations."

"Perhaps a match and some kindling will speed up the process."

Miles couldn't hold himself back. "Sir. You were given a trust to go along with your fortune."

"You forget yourself, Kenway."

"You employed me to care for your property. I am doing my job. *I* do not forget where *my* duties lie." *With Molly and the children, you great idiot.* With that return to sanity, he continued, "Ah, please forgive me, Mr. Gerard." He stood, intending to flee before the Gadabout could gather his thoughts and fire him on the spot. "You are right, I overstepped my bounds and I do hope you understand it is a matter of overzealousness and not disrespect. I have no wish to annoy you or cause—"

"Are you done babbling?"

He gave an inward sigh. "I expect...yes, sir."

"Sit down and finish your damned brandy. We will not discuss my job, although we might touch upon yours."

"Thank you." Miles felt numb as he carefully resettled on the too-small chair. Had he been ushered to such a seat to be reminded he was a clumsy, oversized ox? He eyed the not-too-tall, not-too-large gentleman who employed him, the man who wasn't merely careless but malevolent when it came to his family's building and grounds. He obviously had some sort of grudge against the abbey. What had a pile of ancient stones and glass done to him?

Since his arrival, Miles tried only to gather information from the solicitor, Joey and Mrs. Billings but, assuming he still had a job after this meeting, he would go straight to the Goat and Grape and settle in for some drinking with the local farmers. Surely someone hereabouts would know why Mr. Gerard disliked the place.

Could it be that as a young boy Mr. Gerard had gotten caught in a drafty cell in the old cloisters? Three sides of the original building had crumbled into ruins, but one remained, and some of the tiny rooms in that wing had been preserved and could only be locked from the main hall. Miles imagined the original inhabitants, the monks, had led a harsh life.

He studied the cap he held in both hands rather than raise his head and meet the gaze of Mr. Gerard. Miles hoped his bowed head gave him the air of meekness. Of course Gerard would notice the top of his wild hair and the fact that Miles hadn't had it cut recently, or that he didn't brush his hair nearly often enough. Well, perhaps his shaggy appearance would make him appear a hard worker, although judging from the well-dressed Gadabout, a neat and clean appearance would have worked better in Miles's favor.

"It is rather too late to act as the part of the polite and eager member of staff, Mr. Kenway."

"I know, sir. I am truly very sorry for my bad temper." There. He truly sounded penitent. Earnestly ashamed of himself.

"Huh." The Gadabout didn't seem to believe him. Miles raised his eyes and saw Gerard smiled.

No fine lines at the corners of his eyes—Gerard had great curving lines that transformed his entire face, lifted the gloom from the haunted expression. His smile invited anyone who saw it to return the grin.

Miles's mouth twitched. He wasn't going to relax until he knew he hadn't bullied his employer into firing him.

"To return to the topic at hand."

"The boy?" Miles asked hopefully.

"Your employment."

Ah.

"Your job is safe for now."

"Thank you, sir."

"You are conscientious and mean well."

Indeed I do, you priggish Gadabout. Unlike some I could think of. "Thank you, sir."

Gerard swallowed the rest of his brandy and stood. "I do not need a tour, but we will go hunt down the boy and discuss his future with him."

Now Miles allowed himself a smile. This could be entertaining.

Chapter Three

Unlike the abbey, most of the outlying buildings had been built in the last hundred years. The Gerard family grew and sometimes put older relations or retired servants in one of the several stone cottages not far from the main house, or that was what Gerard recalled.

They walked out into the center yard, along the gravel path. Their steps crunched over gravel and echoed back in that eerie way he recalled now, stone against stone, a sound from boyhood. Walking through the gate to the lawn should have been a relief; their feet were nearly silent on the grass.

They passed the old dairy cottage, and waves of fear suddenly spread through him. His heart wanted to climb up his throat and escape his body.

He longed to run back into the main building, grab up the bottle of brandy and retreat to the library that had once been the monks' refectory.

Beside him, the large bailiff at least had the decency to remain silent, although it occurred to Gerard that he'd rather hear that rich, slow voice than his own thoughts.

"You, ah, like the area?" he asked, trying to keep his tone steady through his queasiness and the tumult of his mind.

The bailiff glanced at him, his large blue eyes widened slightly as if alarmed by the question.

"Of course, yes, sir. I do."

"Do you have family in the area? No, no, of course not. I

recall you said what was left of your family is south of here. During the interview, you mentioned a sister not far away, I think." He could hear himself talking and clamped his teeth together to stop the flow of words. Let Kenway speak.

The trees drew nearer, and he slowed his pace. He felt as if he were Macbeth approaching Birnam Wood rather than waiting for death to come to him. The back of his neck prickled and sweat broke out, unpleasant and chilling, on his body.

Fear. That was all. Nothing more or less. This was no sudden seizure of his heart allowing him to drop dead on the spot—curse his luck. He'd dealt with fear all his life. Simply because this stomach-churning, mind-numbing sensation was fear magnified by a million didn't mean he couldn't stand up to it.

"Sir? Are you all right?"

Damnation, not a bit. He tried to draw breath and realized he couldn't stop himself from pulling in air too hard and fast. His lips and hands tingled, and the air around him seemed to grow dark. Hell and damnation, he was going to collapse and faint like a little girl.

"Something I ate," he gasped, because he'd kill himself before letting the infernal Kenway know he was losing a battle to ridiculous fear.

A large warmth enfolded him—Kenway's arm around his waist, Kenway's body tucked against his, hip to hip, supporting him and pressing him close.

Once, as a very young child in a strange, dark bed in a chamber full of boys, all of whom seemed to hate him, Gerard had pretended a blanket could provide a hug from someone who loved him. He'd wrapped himself in that blanket and was protected by a child's magic. The magic had worked and he'd slept.

Now he could pretend that the bailiff, who was merely trying to stop his ridiculous employer from toppling over, held him firm with true affection and concern. For a moment, he allowed himself to imagine this large, powerful man who smelled of wood smoke and leather and the tang of the outdoors was on his side, literally and figuratively. That thought led to an even more interesting interpretation. He imagined Kenway filled with desire, pulling him close for a kiss. Gerard pictured grabbing him and hauling Kenway so they pressed close front to front.

The blood coursed to another part of his body, clearing his vision. The dark spots vanished. His breath steadied.

He felt as limp as a banana peel after the fruit has been removed.

He felt like an utter prat.

"Thank you," he growled at Kenway, wishing that anyone else—Billings, Joey the groom, even his overreaching valet—had seen this bout of weakness. Not Kenway. He cleared his throat so that the gruffness in his voice might be interpreted as phlegm.

"Better, sir?"

"Yes, I shall be fine. I suspect I haven't eaten enough today and went a bit lightheaded." He pulled away. "Thank you," he added again. "Now where do you suppose the boy is?"

"Shouldn't you return to the abbey? You are quite pale, sir."

He waved a hand and wished it didn't tremble. "It's a passing spell. I am quite recovered, I assure you."

If they didn't march out and face this now, he'd never manage to take this walk. He remembered enough now. Not that he'd forgotten, but he'd never allowed the memory to rise. It filled him. It had never been so strong in the intervening

35

years. This stinking memory was why he could not abide the place. He wanted to push the visions away. He would not allow himself to recall the distorted, purpling face or the blood. Instead, he lectured himself as he had before.

You are no longer a small child. Those people are long gone and buried. She did not hate you. What they did had nothing to do with you.

Blood. Hot, thick blood. Coagulating. That was the word. He saw puddles of it on the stone floor, gallons. But there couldn't have been that much blood. Gerard's brain played those tricks on him again.

He blinked at the images, swallowed hard and aimed his steps so he remained close to Kenway's side. The bailiff couldn't vanquish ghosts. That was up to Gerard—after all, they were his ghosts. Kenway didn't even know they existed, and thank God. But the bailiff could keep him company as he fought his imagination, his memories and his cowardly spirit.

Perhaps every last one of his weaknesses rose from that ancient scene, those cursed flaws.

Kenway would never know, and Gerard would never tell him that they marched into battle now. They would walk around the estate he loathed. They might even take their time about it and he'd recover himself entirely.

As long as they didn't go to the abandoned gardener's cottage, he should be completely fine. "Where has he set up his nest?"

"I believe he's settled into the empty gardener's cottage, sir."

Of course the little blighter had picked the very spot Gerard intended to avoid. Gerard forced a wide smile on his face. "Then we shall pay him a visit."

"He might run off if he sees us, sir."

An excuse to avoid the fear. He would be given a reprieve. He could turn and walk back to the house and visit his dear friend, the brandy bottle. But Gerard would not back down from a skirmish. He cleared his throat again. "Where would he run? There are a limited number of sheds or cottages on the grounds."

Kenway grunted. "As you say." They continued their walk, and Kenway's steps seemed to carry him closer to Gerard. Probably Gerard's imagination.

He considered whistling or humming, two ways he often banished fear, but Kenway already watched him as if he were an animal infected by madness. No need to froth at the mouth. He didn't mind seeming eccentric as long as no one saw the cowardice that formed his weak core.

As soon as Miles said the gardener's cottage, Mr. Gerard flinched as if he'd struck him. And that grimace that followed— a poor excuse for a smile. But at least Miles now understood. The man was held in the grip of fear.

Before that moment, Miles had wondered what ailed the Gadabout who'd sweated and gone pale—perhaps he fought an addiction.

No, he was terrified. Miles had seen fear like this before. Men who'd returned from war sometimes started and flinched and cried out. He knew a man, a soldier during the Crimean War, who snarled and raged at the world every day of his life after he returned from battle.

Mr. Gerard had better control than the soldier, a man who didn't give a damn and said so, often.

Miles considered asking him what was so frightening in these woods, but he'd already been too outspoken and was not going to risk losing his job again. Besides, Mr. Gerard did a fairly good job hiding his emotion now, and no proper Englishman would thank anyone who noticed his weakness. *We are such silly people*, he thought and wished he was back with the larger-hearted and more garrulous Canadians. It must have been the French blood that allowed them latitude in their emotions.

Miles would most definitely walk into the village and find out if anyone knew anything about the abbey's owner.

Clearing the woods of underbrush didn't require extra funds, so he'd managed to keep the paths through the pretty woods open and wide enough so two might walk abreast.

Miles kept a watchful eye on his employer. A few minutes earlier, he'd thought Gerard might faint or vomit, but now he seemed less wobbly. Pale, mouth held tight, shoulders back, poor old Gadabout might be facing a firing squad, but doing it bravely. Miles wanted to clap him on the back or grab his hand and give a reassuring squeeze. Instead, he walked close to the man, close enough to hear his rapid breathing and see the pulse throb at his throat.

Hadn't Molly told him gentlemen were wearing their collars high again these days? Perhaps Gadabout wasn't the first in fashion, although Miles would never guess it. His clothes fit well, showing off his fit form.

"Is something wrong?" Gerard's brows furrowed. "Do I have dirt on my cheek?"

"Not at all."

Miles was glad Gerard's voice had returned to its superior and clipped tones. There was something in his glare and voice that seemed familiar. Of course, without the upper-class accent, Ipsial was the echo and image of Everett Gerard. Two males, each alone against the world, and the world had better watch out for itself.

Miles grinned at the thought. Perhaps the two Gerards would find allies in each other. Heaven knew he'd been trying to reach the young one. Maybe he should try hard to woo the father.

Woo was such an odd word. He bit his lower lip but couldn't shake the new thought. He slowed so Gerard pulled ahead of him to stride along the path.

Now that his imagination had strayed in that direction, Miles had best keep his distance. How absurd that he should suddenly find his employer attractive. He had always had a soft spot for the wounded souls in the world, but never before had he entertained more than sympathy for them.

Gerard stopped and looked back. "It has been years, and I'm not sure of the way," he said as if ashamed of his ignorance.

"Straight on," Miles said jovially and caught up with him.

Chapter Four

One foot in front of the other. He could manage this if he took it in increments. Gerard didn't look ahead at the cottage, which could now be glimpsed between the tree branches. Instead, he watched his own feet move along the path, breaking a twig, rustling through dried pine needles and leaves. Two booted feet walking, bringing him closer and closer to the moment he'd known for years he must eventually face.

Again he was aware of Kenway striding by his side, a large, silent, yet comforting presence. Like a mastiff or a Great Dane perhaps. He nearly smiled at the image.

And then the bailiff stopped walking. "Well, here we are."

Gerard lifted his face, and his eyes were forced to follow to a worn stone doorstep, a weathered gray door with an old-fashioned latch rather than a knob. The building was far smaller than he'd remembered. Just a little square stone structure with small square windows on either side of the door, like two watching eyes.

I can do this, he realized with relief. *Just walk forward like so and lift the latch.* He suited action to words, but as the door swung open into the darkness, a wave of nausea hit him like a strong wind, practically knocking him backward.

Kenway was there again to grab his elbow and steady him. "Sir. Perhaps we should go back to the house so you can eat. You could meet the boy tomorrow after you've rested from your journey."

"No!" Gerard said more sharply than he intended. "We're

here now. I want to go in." He caught his breath and stepped across the threshold.

The interior was cool and dim. Shapes loomed in the shadows, and it took Gerard a moment to accustom his eyes enough to see that they were odd bits of furniture; a low table, a crooked chair, a lumpy pallet on the floor in front of the hearth. No fire burned on the grate and no living figures disturbed the stillness. Oh, but there were ghosts.

Gerard's gaze riveted on the rumpled bedding by the fireplace, and he saw a far different image. The bodies lay exactly as he remembered from all those years ago—the man sprawled facedown with his arm extended toward the woman as if beseeching her, and the woman—face-up. Her tongue protruded slightly between her lips. Her staring eyes, the bright blue gone milky gray, haunted him always. And the blood lit by the glowing embers. The blood he'd stepped in, that he'd found on the bottom of his shoe. His father and then later his aunt told him his mother had gone away, that he had a naughty imagination and hadn't seen anything. He'd almost believed the scene was a dream, but the proof lay on the sole of his shoe, sticky and red.

"Why don't you sit down, sir." Kenway's voice came from far away as he guided Gerard toward the lopsided chair.

"No. Obviously the boy's not here. We should go." Gerard shook off the supporting hand and spun on his heel, just barely restraining himself from bolting out the door.

Once outside, he bent over, hands on thighs, and gulped in great draughts of fresh air. The sharp scent of pine went a long way toward clearing the fog from his vision and calming his thundering heart.

This time Kenway didn't say anything about the condition he was in but stood silently off to one side, waiting for him to recover. Holy Christ, how humiliating to lose control like this, not once but several times in succession in front of the bailiff. The man would think he was a laudanum addict or something, sporadically suffering the fits of withdrawal.

If he'd been alone, Gerard might have collapsed onto the carpet of pine needles, curled into a ball and allowed himself to lose consciousness for a while. Instead, he pulled himself together with an effort of will and straightened, dabbing at his perspiring face with a handkerchief.

"So, where else might we expect to find this boy?" he asked as if nothing unusual had happened.

"As I told you, sir, if Ipsial doesn't wish to be seen, we won't see him. He'll pop up eventually. He always does. Often around mealtimes. Cook sets his meals on the kitchen doorstep, and they're always gone when she goes back for the tray."

"A little ghost haunting the place," Gerard said. "What strange upbringing must the lad have endured to make him act so?"

The bailiff began walking back the way they came, and Gerard fell into step beside him.

"I haven't gotten much information from Ipsial," Kenway said, "but from what little I gleaned, it seems he took care of his ailing mother, Jennie McCray her name was, more than she looked after him. Whether the woman was sick, drugged or mentally incompetent, I haven't been able to ascertain."

"Well, she was sane enough to point him toward the family estate before she shuffled off this mortal coil. I'm surprised she didn't try to get satisfaction sooner, perhaps some aid and support for herself as well as her bastard."

The word sounded unnecessarily harsh, and Gerard wished he could take it back. It suddenly bothered him very much that Miles Kenway would think him irresponsible enough to be sowing bastards in his wake like little seedlings left to tend themselves. However, if he decided to take on the responsibility of Ipsial and raise him as his own son, he could hardly confess to the bailiff that the boy couldn't possibly be his. It must be kept a secret, at least for now.

A flash of movement in the trees caught his attention, and Gerard snapped his head toward it. Something moved on the other side of the stand of trees whose branches arched over the path, something too small to be a deer and too big to be a squirrel or bird. Not to mention too fleshly pale and...navy blue.

"Is that him, stalking us?" Gerard said softly.

"Yes. That's Ipsial."

Gerard paused to consider. If he stopped and called to the lad to come out, he'd likely frighten him away. Ipsial was apparently like a stray dog that could only be coaxed to come near.

Fishing in his coat pocket, Gerard discovered some spare change, a small pouch of tobacco and a tin of sweets he'd used to soothe a recent sore throat. He stopped walking and took out the tin. "Care for a sweet, Kenway?"

Immediately understanding his ploy, the bailiff nodded and in a loud voice said, "Aye. I should enjoy a taste."

The words were innocent, but Gerard couldn't help hearing a double entendre. Apparently he'd spent far too long in the company of flirtatious men, whose words dripped with veiled meaning. The set he'd run with in Italy were flamboyant and bold about their desires and very playful. If Gerard were with one of those men, he would set the hard candy directly on Kenway's tongue, and the man would curl his tongue suggestively around the sweet before drawing it into his mouth and making a great show of sucking.

Gerard could almost see this scene play out, and his cock

Bonnie Dee & Summer Devon

began to rise in response. He shook himself and dragged his eyes away from the bailiff's large, blunt fingers delicately fishing a honey drop from the tin.

Rustling came from the undergrowth, and a sideways glance told Gerard that his would-be charge was coming closer. Gerard loudly enjoyed the sweet. "Mm. Honey. My favorite."

"As a lad, I was always partial to raspberry chews myself," Kenway said.

"I'd eat licorice comfits until the bag was empty, but I got sick on them once and never could abide the things again." Gerard started to put the tin back in his pocket. "Boys do love sweets."

And now the little figure in the woods was only an arm's length away and barely hidden by branches. Without looking directly, Gerard could see a pair of badly worn boots and tattered trouser legs but not much else. First order of business, once he had the boy figuratively eating out of his hand, was to buy him some new clothing. It was shameful that the staff hadn't already seen to that.

Now Gerard pretended to notice for the first time that he and the bailiff were not alone. "Hullo," he greeted the watcher in the wood. "Care for one?" He took out the tin again and held it open on his palm toward the boy.

The little fellow moved out of the trees to stand at the edge of the path. His eyes darted from the candy to Gerard's face and back again, no doubt judging whether he could safely snatch and run. Gerard didn't blink or move but continued offering the sweets.

I'm harmless. You can trust me. I won't grab you or hit you, he tried to telegraph with his eyes. At the same time, he studied the boy's features—the large, pale blue eyes, the sharp, pointed features and the translucently pale skin. Ipsial looked

44

remarkably like the photograph taken of Gerard at about the same age. He'd always appeared ill even though he was perfectly healthy. How well Gerard remembered sitting in the photographer's studio and holding still for what seemed like hours while the man set up and then finally took his image. Gerard still had the photograph in a desk drawer, one of the very few mementos of his past which he'd kept. Why, he wasn't certain, because it only reminded him of that last dreadful summer at the abbey and how horribly it had ended.

Still the boy hesitated. Gerard considering setting the tin on the ground as if tempting a wild animal to come out to feed. But no, it was important the boy take a little initiative and also that Ipsial learned he could trust Gerard.

"You may take two," Gerard said as he slowly crouched to put himself on the boy's level. "But leave the rest please." He would be interested to see if the child would snatch the entire tin or follow his directions. Gerard was aware of Kenway behind him, also holding perfectly still and waiting.

Ipsial came forward, cautious step by step. At first he wouldn't meet Gerard's gaze, but at last he looked into his eyes. The boy was not a halfwit. Keen intelligence lurked in those blue depths, or at least the cunning of an uncivilized savage. *He'll definitely grab the entire tin,* Gerard decided.

"My name is Everett Gerard," he introduced himself. "And your name is Ipsial? That's a most unusual name. I like it."

The lad's arm rose, and a bony wrist protruded from the too-short sleeve of his blue coat. His dirty fingers reached toward the sweets, dove into the box and seized exactly two; then the boy darted back into the woods.

"I hope you enjoy them," Gerard said. "Come to the house and let me know if you do. Perhaps I will give you more."

Seduction by sugar. He'd go to the shop in town and buy

bags of sweets if that was what it took to entice the boy to trust him, and for some reason, it suddenly seemed imperative that Ipsial *should* eventually trust him. Taming the boy was both a challenge and a responsibility. God knew, Gerard had lived without either of those things for too long. Acting the part of a profligate for more than a year had been ultimately unsatisfying. Perhaps caring for this orphaned boy could give him the fulfillment his rootless existence hadn't.

With a creak of the knees, Gerard rose and watched the sea of green swallow up the boy. Only when the branches and ferns stopped swaying did he turn to Kenway. "Timid little thing, isn't he?"

"Timid like a badger," Kenway said dryly. "Don't let his temporary manners fool you. The boy snatches and destroys like a marauding army, although he *has* settled down some in recent days. I suppose he's growing more comfortable here and confident that food will always be available."

Gerard nodded, thinking of the half-starved urchins he'd seen in the slums of London. How horrible that his own second cousin, or possibly half brother, had grown up that way. Who *was* Ipsial's father? There was a short list of suspects, including Everett's own father, who probably hadn't lived like a monk in the many years since his wife's death. But Gerard's money was on Cousin Hubert.

As they headed back toward the house, Gerard's legs felt like lead and his eyes were gritty. He was ready to collapse into bed and sleep for a week.

Before he bid good-bye to Miles Kenway, Gerard impulsively turned to him, hand outstretched. "Thank you for looking after the boy in my absence, and for taking such good care of the property."

For a moment, Kenway stared at his hand; then he took it.

A short, hard shake before they parted. Gerard had once attended a demonstration on the healing powers of electricity and the bailiff's warm, callused palm against his felt surprisingly like the jolt that had touched him at that demonstration. And when their gazes met for a brief moment, as equals rather than master and servant, he felt another pang.

Desire. Lust. He was very familiar with the signal of one man to another. He'd spent a great deal of time with his "own sort" on the Continent, and he recognized that particular look. Great, hulking, manly Miles Kenway desired him, Gerard had no doubt. But what that unexpected bit of knowledge meant to him, he wasn't at all certain.

Chapter Five

After Mr. Gerard walked away, Miles stood staring after him for a good two minutes. He watched the man's neat, trim figure disappear into the abbey, then stared at the door. Had he imagined what just happened or was there really a...spark, for lack of a better word? He felt as if his day had been turned topsy-turvy until he didn't know which end was up. First the unforeseen arrival of Gerard and then his very strange fits, which seemed connected to the old gardener's cottage. Miles had been by turns annoyed and impressed by his odd employer—annoyed by his refusal to take his responsibility as a landowner seriously and impressed by the manner in which he'd coaxed young Ipsial out of the woods. What a confusing mixture the man was.

But most confusing of all were the bursts of attraction Miles kept experiencing in Gerard's presence. He'd taken the man's arm to keep him from falling on two occasions and both times hadn't wanted to let go. As for that handshake... For the master to even offer his hand to a servant was unusual enough, but the sense of a current sizzling between them was something even more remarkable.

Miles was not very sexually experienced. His opportunities for the sorts of encounters he preferred were limited to say the least, but he'd had enough encounters to know what it felt like when desire flared between two men. And he could swear that was what had just happened between himself and Mr. Gerard. What did it mean? Nothing. For nothing could possibly come of it. Ever.

Miles turned away from the abbey and stalked rapidly toward the woods. Like Ipsial, he felt safer alone in the quiet solitude of nature. People confounded him, and while he would occasionally spend an evening visiting with the other servants in the hall, he was just as happy to be by his own solitary fireside.

Tonight, though, he would walk to the village and sit in the pub. He was determined to learn every scrap of information he could about Everett Gerard. Somewhere in this village was someone who knew why the man had virtually fled the estate and was letting it fall into ruin. There was a story there, a bit of history to be ferreted out, and he meant to get to the bottom of it.

The Goat and Grape wasn't very busy on a Thursday night. The barmaid gave him a smile as she drew his glass of beer.

He chose a seat near the fireplace. He smiled and nodded at the village gossip. Miles didn't even have to buy Mr. Reynolds a drink. He paid easily with another sort of coin. The father of the landlord, a retired innkeeper himself, Mr. Reynolds was eager for news about the mysterious young Mr. Gerard.

"We have heard he's making a rare visit to the abbey. A fine-looking young man, I hear."

Miles told him, yes, Mr. Gerard was in residence, and he looked fit enough. He asked Mr. Reynolds, a stout gray-haired man, to sit with him and wondered if he could get more information than he gave about Mr. Gerard.

Miles could only imagine how his employer would respond if news got back to him that the bailiff had retired to the local pub to chatter about the Gerard family affairs. He soon understood he didn't have to worry about his reputation for discretion. Mr. Reynolds apparently preferred to talk rather than listen.

"From what I've heard, he's been quite busy up in London. Mr. Farley was in earlier, and from what he said, our Mr. Gerard has been keeping all sorts of late nights and gadding about Europe."

Miles couldn't help his start at the phrase "gadding about" that echoed his title of the Gadabout.

Mr. Reynolds winked at Miles. "Our Mr. Gerard is a lusty man indeed. He had to have been no more'n eighteen to sire that lad that's running wild about the place."

"Mr. Farley told you about the boy?" he asked.

"No, of course not. We've known about the boy for weeks."

Miles grinned. Of course the village knew about Ipsial. He gave up being discreet and went for direct questioning. "I wonder why Mr. Gerard has stayed away from the abbey. Have you heard any stories?"

A young farmer at the next table didn't even pretend he wasn't listening. With a thump and a scrape, he hitched his chair so he could sit facing them. "The man avoids the abbey because 'tis as dull a place as this village. Nothing happens here or there."

Miles moved back so he could face both Mr. Reynolds and the farmer. "From what I understand, his father, the late Mr. Gerard, rarely visited as well. I suppose both men prefer the city and its excitement."

"Well, now, I don't know why they think we have no excitement here. We do have our yearly fair. And the harvest celebration provides some good fun." Mr. Reynolds sipped his brandy and lemon complacently. "And there are some scandals, of course. The postmistress."

During his very first visit to the inn, Miles had heard ghoulish tales about the spinster who'd been found dead and naked in a married man's bed. He nodded and hoped his face wore the correct expression of solemn interest.

The farmer at the next table said, "Bah. That was years ago. But it was just two years ago Tanner killed his son's wife in a fit of rage." He sounded as proud of the murder as if it made the village a spot of real importance.

Miles had heard about that event as well. He eyed the glass that had held his India ale and wondered if he should drink another or if he'd gotten as much as he could on this visit. "Is there much murder in these parts?"

Mr. Reynolds shook his head but then raised a finger. "There was also the man found dead on the estate, must be fifteen years ago."

"Truly?" He'd heard that story from the housekeeper the first day he'd moved to the area. New to the area herself, she knew little else and the rest of the household staff didn't know details either. "Tell me more."

Mr. Reynold's gray eyes lit up. In a village as quiet as this, he rarely had a new audience. He seemed delighted to share his knowledge, but before he could say more, the young farmer interrupted, "Not fifteen years, more like twenty. Ancient history."

Mr. Reynolds frowned, but apparently not at the interruption. He touched his fingers, and his lips moved. At last he shook his head. "You're right, Jerry, it was twenty years. Time isn't what it used to be. Slippery thing, time."

Hoping to keep Mr. Reynolds from wandering into the philosophical tangent, Miles said, "That must have been interesting for a young boy. A body found near the Gerards' home. Where exactly was the body?"

Could such a discovery affect a man so many years later? It hardly seemed likely. A dead body might be a shock, but the memory of it would hardly turn a strong man into a trembling wreck two decades later.

"They found the man somewhere in the woods. I recall the boy wasn't even at the house when that happened." Mr. Reynolds drained the rest of his brandy and put the tumbler down with a thump. He shot a meaningful glance in the direction of the barmaid, his daughter-in-law. She didn't look up from polishing glasses.

"Everett must have been in school," the young farmer said. "Gentlemen send their boys off to school early."

Mr. Reynolds shook his head. "He'd have been about eight. I think they send 'em away to school about then, don't they?"

Another farmer dragged his chair closer. He piped up, "Wasn't the boy in London with his mother? She spent her time year round there. Never came back here and died of influenza round about that same year."

With some effort, Mr. Reynolds shifted his seat so he faced Miles and his back was to the new interloper. "About young Master Everett, as he would have been then, the story I heard was he was at his aunt's house when the suicide's body was discovered."

"My mum said he'd been murdered," Jerry said.

"No, no. The coroner established that the man, a stranger to these parts, shot himself." Mr. Reynolds rolled his eyes. "I was a man and you were a wee thing back then, Jerry, so I think I can recall the details, thank you."

"May I buy you another, Jerry? Mr. Reynolds?" Miles asked.

"Don't mind at all." Jerry's broad smile made him look even younger than ever. Mr. Reynolds nodded ponderously as if he'd been asked to accept a great honor.

They got Mr. Reynolds's daughter-in-law to draw drinks for all four of them—the other farmer introduced himself as Sandy

Blair. The three long-time residents chatted about the past, but they had very little information about the owners of the abbey.

Mr. Reynolds and Jerry argued over when the last time anyone hereabouts had seen Mrs. Gerard. Mr. Reynolds claimed she'd taken off for London permanently at least twenty years before. Soon after that, news of her death from influenza had reached the village.

They had no more stories about the family, because, as Jerry put it, they were a respectable, dull lot at the abbey, at least until the present Mr. Gerard. He'd shown an interesting side, what with the half-tamed young bastar—young lad of his showing up out of nowhere.

At nine thirty, the public house closed for business, and Miles bid his acquaintances—friends now, really—good night. He strolled down the High Street toward the abbey, which squatted low on the hillside overlooking the town.

Feeling the pleasant hum of just enough drink, he got to the gravel drive and began to sing under his breath, keeping time to the crunch of the gravel under his feet.

"You have a pleasant singing voice, Mr. Kenway."

The voice came from the shadow by the yew hedge. A figure emerged from the shadows and stepped into the moonlight. Mr. Gerard.

Miles hadn't known he was quite so tipsy. But why else would he be striding along the drive up to the main entrance of the house instead of walking along a path to his cottage? And singing "I'll Take You Home, Kathleen", a song that had been popular during his time in Canada.

Seeing his employer and hearing Mr. Gerard's amused drawl did wonders to sober him up.

"Thank you, sir," Miles said.

"Do you sing often or only after drink?"

He clicked his teeth together to stop his own offensive response to the offensive question. "My mother was from Wales, so likely that's how I come by the urge to sing."

"Don't let me stop you. I had just come out into the evening to see if I could track down the young Ipsial by moonlight. He might be tired enough to hold still and actually answer some questions."

"Hmm."

"You don't approve?"

What difference did it make what Miles thought? Gerard was in charge and would do whatever he wished. But Miles had been asked a question, and Gerard was waiting for an answer.

"I think he might feel challenged, sir. I think he'll come along soon to investigate you, if only out of a sense of curiosity. He knows you are in residence and one had only to look at your face to know that you are...you are a close relation of his."

"I don't want to stay at the abbey any longer than I must."

Here was his chance to ask. *And why is that, sir?* But he hadn't had that much to drink.

Gerard said, "You don't approve of that either, do you?"

Miles shrugged. The moon shone bright above the line of trees, so Gerard had to have seen the motion, but he said, "Well?"

"Well what, sir? Do you wish for an argument this evening? I am in a good mood, but you are my employer, and I will oblige if that's what you wish for. I cannot help my opinions, and I am not going to lie about them."

Gerard gave a bark of laughter. "I wonder if I am looking for an argument or some way to relieve tension."

Did the man truly imply...? No, Miles's mind simply took

the journey straight to dangerous, seductive places. He shuffled his feet, a loud noise in the dark.

"What were you doing this evening, Mr. Kenway?"

Mr. Gerard no longer sounded arrogant. In fact, he was almost friendly.

Miles had no trouble answering. "Visiting the village."

"And what are people saying there about young Ipsial?"

So that was the man's trouble. He wondered if he should mention Farley had been spreading news of his own exploits, but for all he knew, Mr. Gerard had sent the valet down to the village just for that purpose. "They seem to know he's connected to your family. But I didn't hear anything more than that." *And why don't you go down and stand the farmers a drink if you're curious?*

He couldn't imagine the upright, clenched-tight figure of Mr. Gerard lazing back on a bench or chair at the pub. The fine white shirt he wore would glow in the dim surroundings of the smoky room. He smiled at the thought of what Jerry the farmer would say to Mr. Gerard.

"Is something amusing, Mr. Kenway?"

"No. Is there anything else, sir?"

Mr. Gerard took a step closer. "I should apologize." Miles had imagined any number of words coming from the man, but an apology was not on the list. He didn't know what to say, and the silence dragged on.

"My indisposition earlier today. I assure you it isn't contagious."

"I know."

"Do you?" And once again Mr. Gerard had reverted to that drawling, amused, forced tone. Worse, he seemed to be waiting for another answer.

"Mr. Gerard, I have seen fear before." Now why had he said that? His employer clearly tried to hide the nature of his malady.

Mr. Gerard's shoulders jerked back and his chin went up as if he anticipated a blow. "Ah." The exclamation came out as a soft exhalation.

Miles waited for the clipped words he had no doubt would follow his effrontery. What possessed him to keep challenging his employer with inappropriate observations? He was practically asking to be let go. The desire to poke at Everett Gerard seemed beyond his control and outside his usual nature. Something about the man roused the devil in him and intrigued him in ways he didn't want to explore too deeply. By all rights, he should apologize for his personal comment, but instead Miles kept silent and waited to see what Gerard would say next.

Chapter Six

Gerard wanted to leap at the bailiff, batter him senseless until he forgot what he'd seen in the woods near the gardener's hut. He wasn't stupid enough to deny Kenway's words. What could he say? It would never do to be seen as spineless and sniveling. No one knew that Gerard had a coward's core—not his father, not Farley, no one but this large man who tried to needle him.

He tried to give a light laugh. To his own surprise, he succeeded. Good. Better than a howl of frustration.

Kenway rubbed a palm over his mouth as if erasing something he might want to say.

Gerard couldn't stand the silence. He longed to find some weakness in Kenway, get him to reveal fear or avarice or impatience.

The bailiff's obvious flaw came to mind. He imagined dragging Kenway into a room, stripping him naked and forcing him to acknowledge his secret unholy passion for men. Too bad he shared that particular weakness and that the thought of Kenway naked instantly aroused him. He laughed again, more naturally this time.

He might have been able to bid Kenway good night and walk away, but then he caught sight of the big man's face and saw sympathy and pity, even in the darkness. Christ, no.

"Do you often have such bouts of fear?" Kenway asked gently.

Gerard's vision immediately went black and red. The

intense fury wiped every emotion, all traces of amusement, away. "This is not your concern," he hissed.

"No, of course not, sir. But it is not so unusual, you know." Kenway dared to take a step closer to him.

"I am not an invalid." Gerard's hands trembled. Strange that anger and fear would have the same effect. He pushed them behind his back, as if coming to parade rest.

"Of course not." Kenway sounded surprised.

"You speak to me as if I were."

"No I don't. Sir."

Much to Gerard's relief, the sympathy had been replaced by annoyance. But he needed more; he craved something dangerous that would erase all memory of his embarrassing fear.

"I'd guess you have about a stone on me, yes?"

Kenway's head jerked back. "What?"

"Yes, at least a stone and an inch or two. But I could take you on in a fight."

The bailiff gave a sharp laugh. "Sir?"

"I'm quite serious. I won't fire you. Even if you knock me unconscious, I won't. Kill me and you might lose your job, but otherwise, I promise it is safe."

"You want to have a bout of fisticuffs? With me?"

"Yes." Any sane gentleman would allow the issue to rest. Already his anger had receded, but the hunger to have at Kenway and show him who was the stronger of them still burned.

"Why?"

Because I want you. Because I have to do something with my body, or I'll go mad with the poison coursing through it. "You

58

are afraid you'll lose? Is that why you're trying to avoid it?"

"I wouldn't lose."

"Ha." Even as he realized how immature, how very silly this challenge was, Gerard felt a bolt of triumph.

"All right, then, sir. Fine." Kenway spoke through clenched teeth. "Where?"

Gerard loosened his tie, took off his coat and vest and unbuttoned his cuffs. "Right here and now would be fine." They were far enough from the house that no one would see them and the likelihood of anyone happening by this late at night was slim. The abbey's grounds were all theirs.

What am I doing? What exactly the bloody hell am I doing? The intelligent part of his brain clamored while his body went through the motions of preparing for a fight. He hadn't had a knockdown brawl since his school days, but he well remembered the sharp pain of knuckles hitting bone and the metallic taste of a split lip. He sized up his opponent, noting the width of Kenway's shoulders when he'd stripped down to his shirt and braces, the muscles of his forearms when he rolled up his shirtsleeves limned in the light of the full moon. This was going to hurt, and he welcomed the pain.

Gerard took a boxing stance, fists raised to protect his face as he bounced lightly on the balls of his feet. Kenway lifted his big hands, also loosely curled into fists, but he made no move toward his employer. Of course he wouldn't. Gerard would have to throw the first punch to demonstrate he really meant to go through with this.

He swung, and his fist connected with Kenway's jaw. Christ. It was like hitting a boulder.

The bailiff's head snapped to one side, but he made no move to hit back.

"Go ahead. Hit me," Gerard demanded. He didn't want a

punching bag but a sparring partner who would give as good as he got.

Kenway gave an almost imperceptible nod, and then his right flashed out and clipped Gerard in the ear. Pain exploded through his head, and he couldn't see for a moment as bright lights flashed in front of his eyes. Gerard shook off the pain and lashed out with an uppercut to the chin.

Kenway didn't hesitate to punch back this time, but Gerard saw the movement of his right hand and danced backward so he received only a glancing blow to the shoulder. It still felt as if he'd been hit by a sledgehammer.

This was a far cry from the boxing he'd practiced over the past couple of years. Gloved for protection and trading measured blows with another gentleman in a gymnasium was nothing like a bare-knuckled barroom brawl or schoolyard fracas.

Gerard landed a blow in the other man's kidneys and surprised a grunt from him. Then he rained a series of punches around the bailiff's upper body before he could recover. God, it felt good to let out his aggression this way. Hand-to-hand combat—as basic and natural as breathing.

Kenway straightened, and the gleam in his eyes let Gerard know he was in trouble. He barely had time to lift his hands to protect his face before the other man attacked. A blow to the solar plexus, and, when he dropped his guard, a punch to his jaw drove him backward. Gerard staggered but kept his feet. When he punched that ridiculously chiseled jaw again, his knuckles felt like they were shattered.

Kenway bobbed and weaved from foot to foot for a moment, regaining his bearings. He lunged forward, and, rather than absorb another series of blows, Gerard stepped in close to avoid them. Their bodies were chest to chest, and he could feel as well as hear the other man's labored breathing—muscle and bone and hot, hot flesh beneath the thin cotton of his shirt. So much heat that for a moment Gerard forgot to fight and simply melted into Kenway's bear hug.

They remained in an embrace for only a moment before Kenway shoved him back and took another swing at him. A hard fist to the gut and Gerard was bent over double, gasping for breath.

"Had enough?" The deep, rasping voice seemed to come from far away as his ears rang.

Gerard forced himself upright despite the pain in his belly. He grinned to show he still could and hopped lightly back. "Not at all."

He lifted his hands and gave a "come on" gesture with his fingers, begging for more of a beating. His bailiff obliged him, rumbling forward like a locomotive and pummeling him around the head and shoulders. It was agony. It was bliss.

Gerard met him blow for blow, landing hits wherever he could. And when he had no air left in his lungs and no strength in his arms, his legs trembling, he collapsed against the other man's body again.

Kenway stopped hitting and once more they stood, swaying together in a primitive dance, neither quite ready to yield or even declare it a draw.

"You...finished?" Kenway asked again, his hot breath brushing Gerard's cheek.

"Are you?" Gerard gasped back. He pulled away enough that he could look the other man in the eyes. Only a two-inch difference between them, so their faces were level, his mouth only a breath away from touching Kenway's. Arousal swept through him, strengthening his already erect cock. Surely the bailiff could feel it through his trousers.

Though the night was dark, there was sufficient moonlight for him to see the gleam in Kenway's eyes, and there was no mistaking the message when his tongue darted out to wet his lips. Rather than pull away from Gerard's erection, Kenway seemed to press more firmly against it. Oh God, this moment was happening, right now, and Gerard felt more excitement at the prospect of a kiss than he had over any man he'd dallied with during his sojourn in Italy. *This* was what true passion felt like.

With another grunt, Kenway dragged Gerard even closer to him and angled his face until their mouths pressed together. Hot lips, wet mouth, a tongue forcing between Gerard's lips and taking possession of him. What little subservient behavior the bailiff might have displayed—which wasn't much at all for an underling—disappeared as he took command of the situation.

Pure bliss. Gerard closed his eyes and surrendered to the sensation for a moment; the strong hand gripping the back of his head, the other pressed against the small of his back and...Christ, the hard bulge rubbing against his. But it wasn't his way to compliantly acquiesce to a kiss. He was more often the one giving than receiving them, so after a moment, he gathered his wits and wrestled for dominance. It was his turn to grasp Kenway's body and plunge his tongue into an exploration of the man's mouth. Gerard was satisfied at the surprised whimper his action caused.

For a long moment, or perhaps a year, it was hard to tell which, they remained that way, locked together and fighting in a different, much more personal way. Then, at last, Gerard pulled back. He drew in a deep breath and muttered the first thing that came to mind. "You taste like cheap ale."

"You taste like an expensive cigar," Kenway countered.

They stood at a short distance, bodies heaving, hands

clenched lightly at their sides, gazes locked and minds assessing each other. *What now?*

Gerard glanced at the yew hedge on their left. He had half a mind to drag Miles Kenway behind it and strip off his trousers and drawers. A quick mutual tug seemed to be what they both needed and wanted. A much better resolution to the evening than a fistfight. Why hadn't he thought of it first?

He glimpsed movement in the shadow of the hedge—an object separate from the foliage—and his heart leaped up to his throat, nearly choking him. He sucked in a breath. "Good God!"

Kenway's head swiveled to look. "Ipsial? Is that you? Come out."

The figure stilled, tried to melt back into the dark shadow, but what was seen could not be unseen.

Panic swept through Gerard as he thought about what the boy had witnessed, something so shocking, so secret, so unacceptable that there were no words with which one could explain it to a child. On the Continent, Gerard had become accustomed to a more permissive bohemian society where men who enjoyed men could relax together with little fear. Now he was drawn back with an elastic snap into the world in which he lived. Such perversion was punishable by prison, and Ipsial had witnessed at least the first step of their union. Who might he tell it to? How could he be cajoled to keep quiet?

Now you understand what Father went through when he tried to make you forget what you saw. The thought dropped like a smooth, cool pebble into his mind and set off a series of ripples. The blood on his shoe. The two still bodies. He'd run away, tearing through the woods where branches whipped his face and blinded him. His father had intercepted him on the forest path, grabbed his arm, demanded an explanation, but Everett had been unable to explain what he'd seen. He'd pointed behind him, stammered something about the gardener's cottage, and his father had left him there in the woods, demanding he remain still. Obedient, Everett had stood shivering until sometime later when his father returned and took him by the arm.

"You will never speak of what you saw today. You will forget it as if it had never happened. Do you understand?" A hard shake accompanied the fierce words and horrifying scowl on Father's face. This was not the father Everett knew, the mild-mannered, distant man who occasionally patted him on the head. This was an angry monster who blamed him for what had happened in the woods.

"I won't. I'll never say a word," Everett had promised, and the secret had become a burden he carried through the years.

Now would he demand a promise of secrecy from a half-wild child who was totally beyond his control? How could he ensure Ipsial's silence? Gerard reached for the jacket he'd discarded on the grass and plunged his hand into his pocket, but there were no more sweets he could offer the boy as a bribe.

"Ipsial, come out *now*," Kenway repeated firmly but calmly.

Slowly the small shadow peeled apart from the larger one as Ipsial moved into the moonlight. Kenway knelt before him but did not reach out to touch the boy.

"It's all right. You're not in trouble. You've done nothing wrong," Kenway assured him in a deep, measured tone that would soothe the fur on an angry cat. "You surprised us. That's all. But what you saw is not to be discussed. Do you understand?"

The boy's head bobbed.

"You understand that a person's private business is his own."

"Yes."

It was the first time Gerard had heard the lad speak. His voice was unexpectedly low for one so young.

"Good man." Kenway gave a nod. "Now, is there anything you'd like to say before we part for the night?"

"Need another blanket," the boy muttered. "Getting cold at night."

"You're welcome to move into the big house if you'd like," Gerard said. "You'd be more comfortable there."

His eyes gleamed in the moonlight. "You have more sweets?"

"Not just yet, but I can pick some up in the village tomorrow. Could you do one thing for me?" Gerard paused. He would not...*not* ask the boy to keep silent about what he'd witnessed. "Will you talk to me for a bit tomorrow? I promise not to ask too many questions, and I promise to provide a most delicious breakfast."

One foot scraped hard at the grass as if the boy would dig a trench. "A'right. I 'spose."

"Good. See you tomorrow, then."

Before the words were out of his mouth, the child had disappeared back into the night.

Gerard exhaled a long breath and turned to Kenway. "Can he be trusted to stay quiet?"

Kenway shrugged. "He talks to no one. Who would he tell? You heard him. He's more interested in creature comforts. If we make no matter of this, neither will he."

Gerard nodded. And now an awkward silence fell between them. There were no words to address what had happened, how a scuffle had turned into a passionate kiss. A kiss that should never have happened. Best to move on as quickly as possible.

"Good night, Kenway," Gerard said stiffly. "We'll discuss

those repair issues tomorrow."

"Very good, sir."

Ah, British formality. How convenient to fall into familiar speech patterns to ignore the explosion that had been touched off between them. Kenway nodded and his, "Is nine o'clock convenient, sir?" held a note of relief.

"I shall see you then." Gerard scooped up and, with unsteady fingers, donned his waistcoat and set off for the house without another look at the bailiff. Not until he reached the sundial near the entrance. Then he glanced back, but it was too late to catch a glimpse of the broad-shouldered man who'd pummeled him, then kissed him until he didn't know down from up.

Gerard leaned against the stone surface of the sundial, feeling the soft moss beneath his palms. "Good Christ. And you thought ghosts were the only things you had to beware of at the abbey."

Chapter Seven

Miles woke from fitful sleep with a blinding headache and a dry mouth. It would be easy to explain away the odd events of last night with a reassurance that he'd been drunk. Trouble was, he hadn't been *that* drunk, only mildly tipsy. And still he'd allowed himself to get into a fistfight—a *fistfight!* for God's sake—with his employer. Then he'd lost the rest of his faculties and let himself get swept away by lust, kissing—*kissing!*—Mr. Gerard. What insanity had possessed him?

He sat up in bed and groaned as his head throbbed. He pushed a hand through his hair and cradled the back of his neck where the tension was worst. A morning-after head wasn't his only damage, as his swollen jaw and aching stomach were also the worse for wear. Mr. Gerard packed a mighty wallop for a gentleman. Not a bad fighter at all. Although why the devil the man wanted to pick a fight with him... Could he be the sort of creature that only gained pleasure when pain was involved?

Miles touched his jaw and winced. He'd never have thought such a thing about himself, yet just the memory of the encounter proved enough to send him into a strange agitation that included arousal.

What is Mr. Gerard's reaction to all this? Is he thinking about me too? Is there a chance that he'll kiss me again?

Good Lord, the girlish voice in his mind must be silenced before he took to wearing petticoats. Men didn't think about whether other men had enjoyed kissing them or not.

Miles threw back the covers and dragged himself out of

bed. A quick wash and shave with cold water soon set him to rights, and by the time his trousers and boots were on, he felt capable enough to march up to the abbey and face his employer once more. What had happened between them would not be mentioned again. That was the manly way. Instead, they would discuss the estate repairs for which the negligent Mr. Gerard refused to pay.

He carefully brushed his hair and picked up his cap. Time to face the consequences of last night. His steps slowed as he made his way from the woods onto the path leading to the house. The gravel under his feet reminded him of that strange interlude.

The fight. Mr. Gerard couldn't fight with himself, so he chose to battle with Miles instead. But that didn't explain the kiss. God. That kiss. He walked faster.

Farley met him inside the servants' hall as he entered and gave him a dignified, "Good morning, Mr. Kenway." He seemed about to pass by but then stopped Miles with a touch on the arm. "Mr. Gerard is in a peculiar mood this morning and apparently had a set-to with some person or persons unknown. He refuses to allow me to summon the local constable and insists it was a matter of mistaken identity."

"Oh?" He longed to ask if that was the extent of Gerard's explanation.

"Yes. Perhaps he was right and we should not have ventured north."

"This is his home."

"He much prefers London and did not look forward to this visit, as you may have suspected. All those letters you sent..."

Did Mr. Gerard share the information with his valet? Miles suspected not. Farley had already struck him as an unrepentant snoop.

Miles would take full advantage of that. He tended not to pry into other people's affairs but decided that Mr. Gerard's antipathy to the abbey could be his business. "Why does he dislike the place, do you suppose?"

"Perhaps he doesn't like the wind or the miles of nothing but low-lying plant life?"

Farley wasn't going to be a source of information after all—but then he added, "I'm not sure why he doesn't sell the abbey. It's no longer entailed. The entailment was broken in his grandfather's generation."

Miles gave a small murmur of interest and then waited. Soon enough Farley said, "I have been in his service these four years, and the last has been, shall we say, quite the experience."

Another questioning hmmm from Miles.

"But I believe that our Mr. Gerard is tired of sowing his, ah, oats and will settle down. Even if he doesn't sell any part of the abbey lands, he has more than enough funds to live a generous existence."

Miles wondered what that meant. He could give away his money to the deserving poor, perhaps?

Farley leaned forward a little. "The boy with the peculiar name. We have come to deal with that situation, as you know. What is that name again?"

"Ipsial," Miles said. He looked at the ponderous clock that ticked at the far end of the corridor. "I have an appointment with Mr. Gerard and am already several minutes late. If you would excuse me?"

Farley frowned, his eyes fixed on Miles's jaw. "You seem to have been in an altercation as well?"

It would never do for the chatty valet to learn the truth.

"No, several days ago I took a tumble from a horse. It's an old bruise."

Farley lifted his several chins and examined him from another angle. "Looks fresh to me."

"I assure you, two days ago. Now if you'll excuse me, Mr. Farley."

"One more thing." Farley touched his arm as he brushed past. The valet glanced around the small hall with an almost guilty expression in his slightly protuberant eyes. His face, always ruddy, grew even redder.

Miles waited, trying to present the less bruised side of his face to Farley's inspection. "Hmm?" He hoped he didn't sound as harrowed as he felt.

"Do you know if the housekeeper, Mrs. Billings, is a widow or married?"

Miles smiled. "Neither. She is a spinster."

"Ah, so I hoped. A title for a most competent housekeeper." His eyes gleamed with another sort of interest.

God speed you with your wooing, Miles thought.

"Mr. Gerard is in the breakfast room," Farley called after him. "There seems to be some sort of leak in the wall of the library. It smells dreadful in there."

Was the leak something to do with the roof or, God forbid, the plumbing? Miles would far rather concentrate on the mundane affair of the water in the wall than in what he could possibly say to his employer. He knocked lightly on the breakfast room door.

"Enter," called Mr. Gerard.

Miles jiggled the cap he clutched in his hand as he opened the door. The table had been cleared of any signs of food or decor. Papers, ledgers and books stood in stacks arranged all around the table.

Mr. Gerard put down a sheaf of papers he held. "No doubt you are wondering why I have turned the breakfast room into a paper depository."

"No, sir. I met Mr. Farley just now."

"Then you are probably well informed. Mrs. Billings discovered a terrible mess in the library this morning. I do not hold it against you that you were right about needed repairs. See how generous I am?"

His eye was blackened, and Miles had trouble looking anywhere else. Even bloodshot that blue eye was beautiful—and that was a useless thought.

"Have a seat, Kenway." He reached behind him for a pull rope and gave it a slow careful tug. "I have also discovered that any sharp pulls might cause the cord to detach itself."

A maid appeared and gave a brief curtsey. Miles didn't recognize her and wondered if Mrs. Billings had been given permission to hire new help now that the master was in residence.

"Two cups and a pot of coffee," Mr. Gerard ordered. "Will that suit you, Kenway? Would you rather have tea?"

"Coffee is fine, thank you, sir."

The maid left and didn't close the door behind her. Gerard frowned, got up and took care of shutting the door himself. Thank goodness he walked easily. Miles distinctly recalled landing a blow that might have created some pain for his employer.

Gerard returned to the chair and rested his forearms on the table, between the stacks. "You look better than I do." He sounded amused—that was another relief.

"I am sorry about your eye, sir."

Gerard brushed his fingertips over his eyebrow. The hint of a smile quirked the corners of his mouth. "That incident... Well. Never mind."

Miles did mind. He wanted to be able to question Gerard as openly as he had the men in the pub or Farley here at the abbey. *What are you thinking now, Mr. Gerard?*

It shouldn't matter to him. Actions, not thoughts or even words, were his concern. And in the long-term, only his employment mattered.

Miles pulled the chair away from the table and sat, his elbows on his thighs, his cap grasped between both hands. He ordered himself not to fidget.

He asked, "Shall I make an inspection of the library and determine what needs to be done?"

"Yes, yes, I suppose. It's one of the oldest sections of this rabbit warren of a house."

Rooms and wings had been added here and there over the centuries. Miles thought the abbey far too spacious for that description, but he said nothing.

Gerard went on. "I inspected the corner of the library, and the trouble seems to be some slate missing from the roof affecting the rooms above. No sewage involved, thank goodness. The smell is old plaster and paper."

Miles half listened and participated in exactly the sort of conversation that should have been held between them months earlier.

Perhaps a thrashing was the best way to make the man behave as a normal, concerned landowner. Although that certainly didn't explain Miles's own response. He'd felt savagely alive as he'd fought. The awareness tingled through him now as he imagined grappling with Gerard, without the blows this time. And without clothes.

"Kenway, are you paying attention?"

"Sorry, sir, my mind wandered."

"Where to?"

He decided a good distraction was required for them both. "About Ipsial, sir."

Gerard leaned back and folded his arms. "What about him? His future or the fact that he might have seen something last night that he shouldn't have?"

"Both, I suppose."

"I must admit I lost some sleep last night thinking." Gerard's expressive mouth tightened. "I won't threaten the boy or allow him to be threatened."

The man was capable of paternal feeling after all.

"Yes, sir."

Gerard stared off into space, his brow furrowed as if he tried to remember something. Miles clutched his hat hard to stop himself from blurting out questions such as *why did you fight me? May we, again?* If it would lead to more kisses, he would be willing to box Gerard's ears.

"Do you suppose he will actually come here for our meeting?"

"You promised him food. That sort of ploy—"

"Call it by its proper name: bribery."

Miles couldn't help smiling. "Yes, that has worked in the past, though not every time I attempted it."

"If you were in my shoes, what would you tell him?"

"About his, ah, possible paternity? I think whatever you could tell him, he'd want to hear." Miles thought he'd tiptoed through that subject nicely.

"And about what he saw last night?"

That was another sticky subject. Miles tried, "Everything within reason."

"Reason had nothing to do with what passed between us, Kenway."

"No, sir." He waited for the stare to move to him, pull him in, but Mr. Gerard continued to focus on something on the wall behind him.

"I should not have challenged you last night, Mr. Kenway." He spoke so softly Miles had to lean forward to hear. "I sincerely apologize."

The hat dropped from Miles's knee to the carpet. He leaned over and fetched it. "No, no need, please."

Mr. Gerard seemed seriously troubled, and Miles wanted to reassure him, as if they were friends. He straightened his back, grimaced at the slight twinge of pain and said, "I don't think it's anything we need worry about. Truth is, sir, I rather enjoyed it. I haven't had a bout like that since I was a child. The fighting, I mean." It would not do to admit to enjoying that hot, unforgettable kiss, the one he suspected would form the basis of many daydreams.

Mr. Gerard finally allowed his gaze to drift to Miles. "No scrapes in Canada?"

"Not for years, sir. I avoid them and others seem to as well. Not since I reached my full height and weight, sir."

For the first time since he'd arrived at the abbey, Mr. Gerard seemed to relax, truly let go of the stick up his arse—and wasn't that an interesting thought.

He unfolded his arms. "If there should be a rematch, we'd have to institute some rules, such as no blows above the torso," he said in his dry, amused tone.

"Certainly, sir."

"That was a jest, Kenway."

"Oh." Miles pulled in a long breath and let it out. "We could bypass the fight then, sir." Let him interpret that as he wished. The jewel-bright eyes narrowed, and Mr. Gerard made a small sound in his throat. Frustration or swallowed laughter.

Chapter Eight

Gerard had not looked forward to this meeting. He was certain he'd encounter a surly, unhappy man who would be ready to make accusations or demand some kind of recompense for his pain or at least an explanation that Gerard had no intention of giving.

Kenway seemed so young now. He blushed as he made slightly lewd statements. And his smile. Good lord, severe men should never smile, because the brilliance of such an expression was too startling—and cut away at Gerard's resolve to keep his distance. If Kenway insisted on flashing that shy, sly smile at him, he'd never properly reestablish their role as master and servant. And that last remark, *bypass the fight.* Accompanied by the smile, Kenway sent the message that he would not mind skipping straight to the delicious aftermath.

Gerard's mouth watered when he thought of kissing Kenway.

The kiss had been as fast and ardent as any he'd gotten from the conte, a firebrand of a man who demanded and gave instant pleasure. No dawdling or games with the passionate Azzari. What would Kenway want from a lover?

Gerard was not a lover; he was an employer. Really, he could not allow himself to daydream in this manner. He had let himself grow too fond of pleasure. He'd not come to the country to dally with another man. That sort of behavior was in the past—his period of debauchery had ended. If he should ever indulge his secret desire again, it most certainly wouldn't be in this small English village that had been his family's seat for generations.

Of course he'd be leaving the area as soon as possible—although that habitual addition to every thought about the abbey no longer felt essential. In less than a day, the fear had been reduced to an unpleasant sensation in his gut, no longer directing his actions. It kicked up as he realized this fact, and the fear seemed to speak to him. *Don't be so sanguine, Gerard.*

Go to the devil, fear, he responded and immediately felt more himself.

He dragged his attention back to the matter of Ipsial. "I should like to get a good look at him," he said.

At Kenway's puzzled frown, he added, "The lad. He's dirty and disheveled, and I expect a good bath would reveal his features."

"One glance and you can see he is a Gerard, sir. No doubt about that."

"Yes, yes, I know." He waved a hand. "But I should like to know if he more closely resembles my cousin Hubert or perhaps my father."

Kenway licked his lips. "Are you saying that you are not... That he's not your son? The mother came from Cambridge, I hear. And isn't that where you were at university?"

"Yes."

"But you don't think..." Kenway picked some lint off his ugly flat cap. "I promise I shan't say a word to anyone, and it is not my business to ask."

"No, it isn't, but go on. Ask if you wish."

Kenway glanced up from his hat and asked, "Is he yours?"

"I won't deny it."

The pale blue eyes seemed to go canny. "*Won't* deny doesn't mean *can't*. It's not true, is it?"

"No, it isn't true." Gerard wondered why he admitted it. "That shall not leave this room, Kenway."

Kenway studied Gerard's face, all traces of the country bumpkin gone now. "You *want* people to believe you have a child out of wedlock, sir?"

"There were rumors back in London. Acknowledging Ipsial as mine would help stamp them out."

"You'd lie about being the lad's father just to stop idle talk?"

"It would help the boy. If I claim him as mine, I can see to it he has advantages in this life."

"Taking on a child like Ipsial is no easy task."

His doubt stung Gerard. He immediately transformed into his old self, the sort who could not bypass the assertion he was doomed to fail. He never passed on a challenge.

"He is a young relation of mine who has been abandoned. I am not head of a very large family—there is only my cousin and his mother left—but I *am* the head."

Kenway might have mumbled something like, "About time you remembered that." Gerard chose to ignore the comment.

"I shall help however I can, sir," Kenway said in a more positive tone. "He has no idea how to get along in the world except by thievery, but he occasionally is more aggressive—"

"Aggressive?" Gerard repeated. "Oh, of course, there were the stones he threw at me. The little blighter might have hit my horses. What else has he done?"

"There have been accidents, but I have seen no real malice in the lad."

"The stone throwing was no accident."

"I suppose he felt threatened." Kenway sounded uncertain.

78

"There are two of us, grown men, Kenway. We will prevail over one scrawny, unhappy boy, particularly if we use bribery."

"Call it a ploy to win his favor, sir," Kenway suggested with a smile.

Gerard began to laugh and had trouble stopping even after the two maids brought the trays of bread and coffee into the breakfast room.

"I shall go now, sir." The bailiff rose, and the spindly chair creaked at the loss of his weight.

"Nonsense. Please join me for breakfast. Sorry there's nothing hearty like kippers or sausage, but I've become accustomed to the lighter fare." Gerard nearly held his breath, he so hoped the man would stay to eat with him.

For a moment, as Kenway twisted his cap in his hands, Gerard feared he'd lost him. Kenway would make an excuse about seeing to his duties and leave. But instead, he gave a curt nod and resumed his seat. Gerard was inordinately pleased. He dismissed the maid and poured the coffee himself.

With the ancient, heavy draperies pulled back from the windows, the sun shone through the many panes, and dust moats glittered in the beam of light. The wallpaper, rugs and furnishings of the room were worn with age but at least clean, thanks to Mrs. Billings's expert care of the house. Given a freshening up, Gerard could see the potential for beauty in the room. How much money would it take to bring the entire building up to snuff and make it hospitable enough to entice a buyer? He handed Kenway a plate and steaming cup and was about to broach the topic, when there was another knock on the door.

Mrs. Billings entered. "Pardon me, sir. Young Ipsial has said you wish to see him this morning?" She sounded as if she didn't believe this could possibly be true.

A second later, a grimy imp popped up beside her. His nearly shoulder-length brown hair stuck out in all directions, rather like Gerard's own when he woke in the morning, but there appeared to be leaves and twigs protruding from the wild mane. The boy's thin face was dirty, his eyes avid as they swept over the tray of breads and scones. He started toward it.

Mrs. Billings started to reach out as if to pull him back, then seemed to think better of it. "Master Ipsial, you should wait for an invitation to enter a room."

Her words went unheeded as the boy grabbed up a slice of toast, rubbed it over a slab of butter, then took a huge bite.

Gerard considered his options. Attempt to discipline the boy about manners, or continue to try to woo him with sweets? He went for the latter. "Thank you, Mrs. Billings. You may leave the boy with me."

Tight lipped and shaking her head, the housekeeper turned and walked out, her rigid shoulders a picture of indignation.

Gerard exchanged a look with Kenway as the boy continued to gorge himself for several moments. Kenway seemed as if he'd like to reprimand the boy himself, but he kept silent and deferred to Gerard's authority.

"A little hungry today?" Gerard asked Ipsial. "Why don't you take one more piece of toast, then come sit over here and talk to me?"

Ipsial cast a sidelong glance but did as he was bid, scuffing across the carpet and plopping down on a sofa. A fainting couch it was called, and Gerard suddenly had a very clear memory of his mother sprawling on that dainty chaise. He saw her laughing and reaching out to him, and he remembered the rose scent when she hugged him tight against her softness.

For a moment, he couldn't breathe as an ache seized his chest. But he forced himself to inhale and meet Ipsial's frightening blue eyes. They were clear and wide, almost protuberant, and gave the impression that the boy could see deep inside a person. Or maybe the poor child was simply nearsighted and could use a pair of spectacles.

"So Ipsial, I understand your mother sent you here to find me," Gerard said. "I'm sorry it took me so long to receive the message and return home." He couldn't resist glancing at Kenway, whose lips tightened in annoyance. "Mr. Kenway here sent me many a letter about you, but I'm afraid I missed my correspondences for a time. But I'm here now."

Crumbs littered the front of Ipsial's shirt, and his jaw worked as he continued devouring toast. He stared and stared, and Gerard wondered what thoughts darted through his mind.

"You understand that I may be your father?" He still wasn't certain he was ready to claim Ipsial as his own, but he would speak in oblique half-truths for now.

"Yes. That's what Mum said." Again, the boy's low, almost rasping voice was unexpected. "She said, 'Go to the abbey' and told me how to get here. She said Mr. Gerard was to look after me."

"I see." Gerard nodded, growing more certain by the moment that he was facing his very own half brother, progeny of his father's waning years. Yet it seemed so out of character for the man. "If your mother said I should look after you, then I suppose I must. Can you tell me more about her?"

Ipsial cocked his head and stared even harder. "You knew her, din't you?"

"Let's say I need a reminder. Describe what she looked like."

The boy shrugged. "Like a mum." Then he added more thoughtfully. "She had nice brown hair until she got really sick. Then it mostly fell out."

Gerard winced. "I'm sorry to hear that. You don't have to talk about her. I understand if you don't wish to be reminded of your mother. I too lost my mom when I was about your age. I missed her a great deal, and it was painful to think of her."

"My mum had the wheezes. What'd yours die from?" Ipsial asked conversationally.

"An infection of some sort." Gerard repeated the lie he'd been told all his life. "It took her very quickly." Again he glanced over to Kenway. The man's eyes were narrowed as if he doubted the truth of Gerard's words. Perhaps rumors abounded in the village even today.

"At any rate," Gerard said, anxious to turn the topic to less morbid channels. "You're here now, and I should be glad if you stayed. Perhaps we can get to know each other better."

"He"—Ipsial stabbed a finger in Kenway's direction— "promised to teach me to shoot. Do you know how to shoot?"

"Not very well, I'm afraid. I've no use for guns."

"Oh." The boy's expression lost its momentary gleam of interest and resumed a habitual guardedness.

"I suppose I could learn along with you. What about this morning, Mr. Kenway? Are you too busy, or could you give us a shooting lesson?"

Ipsial perked up. "Right now?"

"Aye, I imagine I could make the time," Kenway drawled. "Must stop by my house to collect my guns."

Gerard perked up too, excitement simmering at the idea of spending time with Kenway as well as seeing the man's residence. In fact, his excitement far exceeded the circumstance. He really needed to get his emotions under control.

"I shall change into something more suitable and meet you

at your house," he said casually.

"There are a couple of pistols in a case in the study if you care to bring them along," Kenway said. "Beauties, both of them, but they likely need a good cleaning. I don't know how long since either has been fired."

Gerard had a guess but doubted if he was right. His father had probably disposed of the murder weapon in the boggiest part of the grounds. It would be insanity to have kept the gun on display all these years.

Gerard parted from Ipsial and Kenway and went to change from his morning jacket into more casual attire. Then he went to his father's study, which was exactly as he recalled it from his youth, and stared at the case where two large pistols lay, gleaming against a burgundy felt background.

He stared at the weapons for a good two minutes but couldn't bring himself to unlock the case and touch either one. He headed outside, still thinking about his father.

Kenway's cottage was as quaint as a fairy tale with its mossy roof and stone walls, a cozier echo of the grim main abbey building and nothing like the dilapidated abandoned hut in the woods. Before Gerard could knock on the door, Kenway stepped through, ducking his head to clear the lintel. His big shoulders filled the doorframe, and Gerard wondered if the man also dwarfed the furniture inside. What was his bed like? Was there room in it for two? And, damn, he had to stop thinking things like that.

Kenway carried two weapons, dangerous-looking things with polished wood stocks and gleaming barrels. Noticing that Gerard had not elected to bring the pistols in the study, he offered him a shotgun.

"No. No thank you."

"'Twill be hard to learn to fire if you won't handle the weapon."

"That's all right. I'll watch you and Ipsial and look on this as an opportunity to spend time with the boy."

As if conjured by his name, Ipsial popped out of the cottage behind Kenway. He carried a couple of boxes of shot and a canteen slung over one shoulder.

"One's a rifle, the other is a shotgun," Ipsial informed Gerard. "I'll carry a gun. I know how to hold it properly. Mr. Kenway showed me." The boy was more animated than Gerard had yet heard him.

"All right, then." Kenway handed him the shotgun, muzzle pointed toward the ground. Ipsial flipped the heavy weapon to rest the barrel against his shoulder.

"What did I tell you was the first rule of handling a firearm?" Kenway asked.

"Check to make sure it's not loaded. But you wouldn't have given it to me if it was."

"Doesn't matter. *Always* make certain. Never assume."

Gerard appreciated the gravity with which Kenway treated the matter. He had some concerns about a mercurial boy like Ipsial taking shooting lessons, but perhaps it was for the best. Ipsial did as he was told, resting the stock against his shoulder and checking for shot in the chamber. "Clear," he announced after he'd snapped it back together.

Kenway led the way to an open glade, away from the windows of his house, and set up some targets for them to shoot at. He placed several gourds from his garden along the top of a fallen tree trunk. Their bright oranges and yellows should make them an easy target. He talked Ipsial through the process of loading the weapon and demonstrated on his own.

"Now. Rest the butt against your shoulder. Brace your legs like so. Arms steady. Breathe slowly. In. And out. Now rest your finger on the trigger. Lightly! When I tell you to, you will exhale, then squeeze—not jerk. Accuracy is all about remaining calm and controlling your breath."

It sounded like a lot of instructions all at once. Gerard noted Ipsial's arms trembling in an effort to support the obviously too heavy rifle. But the boy's jaw tightened and he braced his legs as Kenway had shown him. His chest rose and fell as he sighted down the barrel. Gerard held his own breath, waiting.

"Now squeeze," Kenway ordered.

Gerard jumped as a loud boom echoed in the clearing. Ipsial staggered back from the recoil. None of the gourds were disturbed from their places on the great log.

Kenway rested a hand on Ipsial's shoulder. "That's all right. You need a smaller weapon to learn on, but soon you'll be able to support the weight."

"And we can go hunting?"

"Perhaps." The bailiff shot a look at Gerard, and it was easy to read the question in his look. The man didn't want to make a promise to the boy that he couldn't keep, not knowing how long Ipsial would be living on the estate.

"Your turn," Ipsial said, resting his rifle on the ground as Kenway had taught him.

"Very well."

Gerard was mesmerized by Kenway's smooth, efficient movements as he lifted his shotgun and sighted down the barrel. Two quick shots and two gourds exploded in a shower of pulp. Gerard winced, hating the sound, but Ipsial crowed in delight.

Then Kenway crouched beside the boy and gave him further instruction, this time supporting his frame as he prepared to shoot. Gerard was moved by the bailiff's patient, fatherly manner, something his own boyhood had been severely lacking. He braced for another report and managed not to jerk this time as the bullet bit a chunk of bark out of the log.

"Not bad," Gerard said.

Ipsial glanced up at him. "You want to try?"

No. Not at all. Not ever. But the boy was actually responding to him, including him, and he couldn't refuse. "Certainly. Can you show me what to do?"

He accepted the rifle from Ipsial and followed his directions as the boy explained step by step exactly what Kenway had just taught him. The weight of the rifle and the scent of burnt gunpowder made him feel vaguely ill, but Gerard never backed down from a challenge. He raised the rifle, focused on one of the gourds and squeezed the trigger at Ipsial's command.

The explosion in his ears was followed by a small branch evaporating in a shower of leaves.

"You hit something. Good!" Ipsial complimented him.

Gerard exchanged a look with Kenway over the boy's head. Evidently Ipsial had the ability to act like a civilized being and demonstrate some good manners.

Gerard surrendered the weapon to Ipsial, then stepped back and observed while his two companions took a few more shots and decimated a few more gourds.

"Enough for today," Kenway announced shortly. "You'll have a bruise on your shoulder by tomorrow."

"M'ears feel like they been boxed too." He looked up at them. "I don't look as bad as you do. Which o' you won the fight?"

"Where did you learn to shoot?" Gerard asked Kenway, ignoring the boy's question.

"I grew up hunting with my father in Yorkshire, bringing home game for the table. And when I moved to Canada, there was plenty of hunting there."

"Did you ever shoot a bear?" Ipsial demanded.

He smiled. "No. Only deer and rabbits. Not so much as a moose, although I saw one on occasion."

Gerard pictured Kenway as a boy and imagined he'd been a big, raw-boned lad, striding along beside his dad and gutting deer like an experienced butcher. He wouldn't flinch at the sight of blood or jerk at the sound of gunshot.

"How many in your family?" Gerard asked, curious to know more about the background that had shaped the man.

Kenway snapped the two pieces of rifle together and smoothed his hand over the stock. "I had three siblings. One brother died young, from a fever. My other brother died in an accident several years ago. All I have left is my sister, a widow, and a niece and nephew. My parents also passed away in an influenza epidemic."

"I'm so sorry," Gerard said. Now he recalled a few of these details from their brief interview in London. "You returned from Canada to help your sister, yes?"

The bailiff nodded. He suddenly frowned. He'd been squatting, but now he jumped to his feet, snarling. "And where do you think you're off to?"

Ipsial was close to the edge of the clearing. He backed up, fear in his eyes. In three short strides, Kenway got to him and grabbed his skinny arm.

Gerard was astonished at Kenway's manner and was about

to shout a protest when the man held out his other big hand, palm up.

"Give," he ordered.

The boy reached into his rags—Gerard would have to find a way to get new clothes for the boy. He pulled out some of the bullets for the rifle and a load of shot.

"What do you think I should do now, eh?" Kenway growled at the boy.

"Nothing?" Ipsial tried. "I was just going to borrow 'em."

"Those are dangerous, Ipsial. What's more, taking something without permission is called stealing. Not so very long ago, a boy could be put to death for such a thing." Kenway sounded calm now, but he took the bullets and, still dragging the boy, walked over and sat the boy down on a stump. "My da would have beaten my backside until I couldn't sit down."

Ipsial squeaked and lunged forward as if he'd bite Kenway to force him to let go.

"Here now, Kenway," Gerard began.

Kenway didn't appear to notice him. All of his attention was directed at the boy. "I won't do that. But tha' mun pay a price, lad. No. More. Thieving."

"I won't."

"Swear it, boy."

"I won't, I promise."

"You know how to tell time?"

Ipsial nodded.

"I'll let you go for now, but in four hours I shall meet you by the clock in the stable yard. You will be ready to work."

"Work?"

"Yes. Work. If you do what I say, I'll consider offering you more shooting lessons. If you do not, I will find you. I will tell Mrs. Billings to set out nothing but gruel for the next month. Four hours. We'll meet by the old clock on a pillar next to the stable yard."

He let go of the boy, and Ipsial fled as if he'd been shot from one of the guns they'd just been using.

Gerard shifted his attention away from Kenway's back and haunches. "We must not allow that boy to get his hands on a deadly weapon."

"Yes, sir. I shan't be able to keep them in my cottage. T' lock is broken."

"We can lock the weapons in the abbey's gun room." He moved through the glade, ducked under a low branch and waited for Kenway to follow.

As they walked toward the house, Gerard asked, "Why did you give him four hours? I always assumed one should treat a child like an animal, make the punishment fast and immediate so he will associate the deed with the consequences."

"Perhaps you are correct. I wished to give him time to think." He'd lost the touch of the local broad accent again. It seemed to appear only on occasion. "If he chooses to appear, then I know I've got some control over him." Kenway gave a short bark of a laugh. "And truthfully, it will give me time to think of what I can do with the young fool. Ah, and I shall discover if he really does know how to tell time. He's ignorant of so many things."

Gerard snorted. "I have heard children described as a blessing."

"Yes, sir. My niece and nephew are indeed well-behaved children."

The idea that popped into Gerard's head seemed absurd at first. He'd be adding kerosene to a fire. But he found himself voicing it anyway. "This lad is not fit for a school or society. Perhaps a proven child tamer might be able to assist us."

"Is there such a thing, sir?"

"Your sister apparently knows how to raise children. Perhaps we should take advantage of her experience."

Chapter Nine

Miles stopped in his tracks, wondering if he'd heard correctly. "My sister, Molly—I beg your pardon, I mean my sister Mrs. Trentwell. She is a good mother. Yes."

"How would it be if she came here? I'd be willing to pay her a salary."

Miles had to clear his throat. "I'm sure she would be glad to do so, sir. I would be grateful." That hardly began to describe his feelings. Gratitude, fear—if his family came here, they would finally have a decent place to live. Yet if he lived near them it would be that much more difficult for him to run away.

"Very good," Mr. Gerard said briskly. "We'll put the guns away and discuss the matter."

He led the way to the back of the abbey, a small door that led to the colder and dustier portion of the rambling structure.

Gerard strolled past the former monks' cells and the tiny secondary chapel, and Miles decided that his employer's previous display of fear wasn't linked to the ghosts of long-gone residents of the abbey.

They went through a thick oak door that must have been an exterior exit at one time and entered the newer, larger portion of the building.

Mr. Gerard hesitated for a moment. "The place is a maze."

"To the left, I think?" Miles knew, of course, but didn't want to show off his superior knowledge to his employer.

"Of course." Gerard walked across the hall to the room that

held a billiard table and, in the corner, an enormous, ornate cupboard.

He went to the cupboard and swung open the double doors. Inside was a jumble of weapons. On the bottom of the cabinet lay three shotguns, a pistol, epees and sabers—and several billiard cues. Miles winced to see the disarray. "Might I, uh…" He looked at the doors and saw each held racks that must have been the proper storage place for the shotgun and epees. "I should like to tidy this, sir."

Gerard leaned down and touched the blunt end of a fencing epee. "My father must have left the cabinet like this. I hardly care about it, but certainly, you may straighten it out, later on. Put your weapons anywhere you choose. The lock is on the door to the room, not the cabinet."

He went to the door and turned the iron key in the lock, then tried the door handle. "Good. It works," he said.

And then Mr. Gerard pocketed the key.

"Ah, sir? The door?"

Gerard smiled at him, showing all of his white teeth. "The door is locked. And this is the only key." He patted his pocket. "Shall we play billiards? No one will see any games we should decide to play." He almost purred the words.

Miles licked his lips. The invitation seemed obvious to him, but if he heard wrong, God above, what a terrible moment that would be. He would not make any moves.

"Shall we discuss my sister coming to the abbey?"

Gerard's smile froze a little. "I'd rather do other things just now."

Miles would not lower his gaze. He forced himself to keep it focused on his employer's face. His mouth was dry again. He ran a hand over his lips. Gerard watched.

"With your swollen eye and my aching side, I don't think it would be wise. A rematch, I mean."

Gerard laughed. "No, indeed." He walked over to Miles and brushed a finger over his swollen jaw. "I regret marring your appearance."

It was Miles's turn to laugh. "Yes, I'm such a model of perfection."

For the first time in several long moments, Gerard's smile vanished. "Indeed you are," he said.

Miles had forgotten how tall Gerard was, only an inch or two shorter. He was not used to being so close to a person and looking them directly in the eye. Such gorgeous eyes too, even with that distracting, distressing bruise around the one.

The pressure of that gaze traveled through his body down to where it gathered power, and he knew from the brush of cloth that he grew erect. His breath—he couldn't control it, and each breath seemed to break in a gasp now. He would not move.

This could be a trap. Gerard might strike him. He waited for the strange tension to grow or break or...

He would grow mad in the long seconds of anticipation.

Gerard came so close Miles felt the warm exhalation on his cheek—and still neither of them spoke or closed the distance between their mouths.

Somewhere in the building, a clock tolled. Even such a distant sound made the jumpy Miles start.

Gerard's hand rested on him. "Shh," he soothed as if Miles had become truly agitated. The weight of the hand on his shoulder did nothing to reassure him.

To the devil with it. If he was going to go to hell, if he was going to lose his job, so be it. He turned his head, closed the last few inches and lightly pressed his mouth to the other man's parted lips. No awkward fumbling, no clashing—this time his aim was as perfect, as if he'd practiced the touch of a delicate kiss.

The effect was instantaneous. Gerard moaned and gripped his shoulder hard. The mouth under Miles's moved, softened, opened and *thank you, thank you,* the damp sweep of a tongue touched his lips. He bent his head to the side so that their mouths fit and ah, they did, perfectly.

Gerard's hand moved up, cupping his skull, holding him in place. Miles grew bold enough to reach under the fine woolen jacket and run his hands up and down, feeling the scrape of impossibly soft satin lining on his knuckles and the muscular back under his palms. Gerard's form was strong and thin, elegant yet essentially male.

The horrible reality of his maleness only made Miles harder and more restless to touch him, to feel the quality of his skin. Gerard pulsed against him, his cock pushing against Miles's groin.

Gerard reached down and drew his hand up and down Miles's erection, both of them groaning at the touch.

A touch of air brushed over Miles's belly, distracting him from the deepening hungry kisses. Mr. Gerard had unbuttoned his trousers and had slid under his shirt and waistcoat. Long, skillful fingers reached beneath the band of Miles's trousers and rubbed his cock. Each stroke seemed teasing, a promise of more. When Gerard at last grabbed him full in his fist, Miles's groan filled the room. He reached blindly down Gerard's side, across the flat stomach to trousers and fumbled with his buttons.

This! Giving in to the endless hunger and need. Christ, the feel of the man bucking, insistently shoving against his palm.

The scent of a pampered man, the harsh breath and soft groan. So much slender perfect man for him to touch. He wanted to drag off the coat and waistcoat, push down the braces, shove off the trousers so he'd get to touch all of that cock more easily. See it too. Maybe even press his nose close to the thatch of hair and take the mouthwatering cock in his mouth and cover it with licks.

With a warning cry, he erupted.

Gerard's hand didn't slow or stop but demanded every shuddering spasm and held Miles firm until the last twinges reminded him that he should repay such a pleasurable favor.

He pulled in a long sigh that seemed to increase the satisfying contentment radiating from his spent balls out to his fingertips and toes. All of him rejoiced.

Then he dropped to his knees and burrowed his face into the mass of clothes, using his hands to seek out Gerard's surprisingly large cock, the balls already drawn tight.

It wouldn't take long, only a lick and a suck, but he wanted to enjoy this experience. He hadn't done such a thing with other men, but he had such a very strange relationohip with Gerard. From fighting for no reason to this. Never mind that the man now stroking his hair, softly whispering obscenities, was his employer. No one else would inspire him to such greedy depths.

Incredibly, his own interest stirred again.

He craved more and opened his mouth to engulf as much of the blunt, hard erection as he could. Sucking and licking, he explored the weight and girth of the cock with his lips and tongue. Gerard rocked now, pushing in, drawing away. His organ was surprisingly large for such a slender man. The rough cloth of his trousers brushed Miles's chin. Not an irritant, but it reminded him he wanted to be able to do and touch more.

He reached for the buttons that fastened Gerard's braces to

his trousers. That required two hands, so he pulled back, ignoring Gerard's whimper of a protest. Once he understood what Miles wanted, Gerard backed away at once and scrabbled at his clothes.

"Yes. Wait," he gasped. He pulled off his jacket and waistcoat and pushed his braces off his arms so that his already open trousers dropped around his ankles.

Miles sank back on his heels and grinned up at him. "With your feet entangled like this, it would only take a little push and you'd topple over."

Gerard winced. He backed up and rested his naked bottom on the billiards table, his two hands grasping the edge as if he held on to a bouncing wagon. He pushed his hard cock forward. "You did seem to be enjoying yourself. Far be it for me to interrupt your pleasure."

Miles's grin grew. "My pleasure, but you don't mind it, I think." He moved forward on his knees and took the damp erection into his mouth again. He reached around, and Gerard, still clutching the table for support, obligingly shoved his buttocks up so Miles could have the pleasure of grasping his firm arse with both hands, squeezing the muscular and satisfying curves as he sucked.

Gerard gasped. "So warm. Yes. God, please." He shoved forward and back almost desperately. Miles had to release one hand's grip on the sweet arse to hold on to the demanding, pumping organ invading his mouth.

In less than a minute, Gerard's cock swelled and grew even harder in Miles's mouth and grip.

He cried out, "Now," and the thrum of his spending sped through his cock and shot into Mile's mouth and throat.

Miles had intended to pull away, catch the ejaculate in his handkerchief, but the flavor was not offensive. He kept his mouth in place, swallowing and lapping.

Gerard pleaded, "Please, please." He cried out with every throbbing burst and continued to beg as Miles carefully licked him, then used his handkerchief to dry him off.

"My God," Gerard gasped. "Where did you learn such a thing? Canada?"

"Here. With you." Other than a lick or a kiss, he'd never taken that part of a man into his mouth before. Not with so much deliberate pleasure.

"You..." Gerard pushed himself away from the billiards table. He hauled up his trousers and straightened. "You have a natural turn for the work. My God," he repeated for perhaps the fifth time. "I'd say you should hire yourself out for it, but I know it's a dire insult to propose such a profession."

Miles stuffed his handkerchief into his back pocket and rose to his feet. "It is," he said. Now, while Gerard still had the afterglow of pleasure, Miles had to speak his mind quickly. "I do work for you, but what I did will never be a condition of my employment."

"No, no, Kenway. I hope you understand I am only grateful. I have no wish—"

Miles interrupted by moving close and kissing him on the mouth. Not a greedy, thrusting kiss, just a small brush of the lips. Only as he drew away did he realize it was the kiss of an affectionate lover, but he wasn't going to worry about such things.

"Yes. I understand, sir."

"You can't call me sir. Not after that. Not..."

"I can and I should. Sir. What we did was an aberration, a moment of self-indulgence."

Gerard thoughtfully tucked in his shirt, buttoned his

trousers. "I comprehend your meaning, I think. You don't want such a thing to happen again, and we should carry on as if it hadn't.' "

Miles wondered if that was indeed what he preferred. He rubbed his eyes. "I cannot say what I want, for when you and I are together, the strangest things seem to occur." He added after a few too many seconds later, "Sir."

Gerard laughed. "You are the reason for the strangeness, I believe. One moment you're the picture of an obedient servant, almost a clodpoll of a man; the next you are ordering me around, and then sucking me off like the most skilled... Never mind that. Not an insult, I assure you, only praise." He reached for his waistcoat, buttoned it closed, still moving slowly as if reluctant to cover his skin. "You are a mystery to me, Kenway."

Miles watched, licked his lips, barely listening. He'd never seen a body that appealed to him more, and he'd barely been able to touch it, so his hands still longed to discover the roughness of hair he'd only glimpsed on Gerard's torso. And that bottom. He'd give a half year's salary to explore the dip where Gerard's spine met those perfect globes. He'd use his mouth again. That was so delicious—

"Kenway. You appear to be hungry. Shall I order more food?"

"I am not hungry for food."

"My God." Gerard's voice was low and rough. "You are amazing. I knew a man, a count, who appreciated passion, but you put him to shame. And what was it you said about the moment out of time? We will not do this again, I think you said or at least implied."

That's right. Miles had indeed insisted on saying such a thing. Was it a full two minutes ago? He'd been stunned with pleasure, with the sharpening of desire and its release. But once the aftermath of pleasure dissipated and he was alone, the remorse would start.

No shame, he reminded himself. He had no use for that sort of humiliation when it came to his appetites. At least no more than was necessary to stop himself from acting out again. Christ and with his *employer.*

"Kenway. What is your given name? Miles, that's right. Miles, give over the worry. I see it in your expressive face. What is done is done. Now we shall plan our future, or rather Ipsial's. Recall we were to discuss the possibility of bringing your sister the lion tamer here to help us with our cub."

Miles blinked. "Yes. That's right." Could such a thing be a good idea? Seeing Molly every day and her little ones. Yes, of course. He missed them more than he allowed himself to think about, usually.

But what about Mr. Gerard? No doubt he'd return to London and his regular life. Once again, he wondered why Gerard, who clearly hated this place, didn't simply sell. Perhaps all those generations weighed down on a man, stopping him from making rash decisions about property that held his ancestors' bones.

If Gerard went away again, Miles would be able to return to his life and work. He'd been more than content—he'd been happy with his employment and the area. The only regrets he'd had were that he couldn't seem to reach Ipsial and that his remaining family wasn't nearby. With the plans they might make now, both regrets would be eliminated. He could be happy, even happier than before.

When Gerard left, he'd sink back into his life. When his employer left... Miles suddenly understood that he'd be bored and lonely, a condition he recalled from his first long Canadian winter. Usually when such restlessness hit him, he moved to his next situation.

He wanted to bury his face in his hands or curse out loud. His pleasant, solitary existence had been turned upside down and inside out by several interludes with Mr. Gerard. He'd been changed by their interactions. Now he simply had to shove all those changes away and transform himself back into the man he'd been before Gerard erupted into his life.

Chapter Ten

Gerard felt as if he'd been caught up in a whirlwind, spun around and dropped back down to earth. He'd arrived at his family home, full of trepidation and cobwebbed fears. He'd swept away those old cobwebs, to an extent, and unexpectedly discovered pleasure in a place he'd been sure would only hold misery.

Miles Kenway. A solid boulder of a man. Salt of the earth. Upstanding and responsible. And as bent toward relations with men as a Greek. Who would have guessed it?

And Kenway wasn't the only good thing to be found at the abbey. Gerard was greatly interested in taming Ipsial. It was a challenge and a responsibility, and God knew, he'd had precious little of either during his fallow time of pursuing entertainment. He was ready to dig in and see what he could do with Ipsial—and with the family homestead. Whether with an eye toward selling or merely to bring the place to a more habitable condition, he was ready to assume his responsibilities as an owner.

"Kenway," he said, straightening his jacket. "You had a list of repairs the house needs. I'm ready to discuss those improvements with you."

"Yes, sir." The bailiff's polite tone was back in place, as if they hadn't just had their hands all over each other. How strange to move from such intimacy to that distance of master and servant. Kenway might be fine with the shift, but Gerard needed time alone to compose himself and regain his footing.

"Why don't you attend to whatever duties you had previously scheduled for this afternoon and come to me after dinner with your suggestions?"

"Yes, sir," Kenway repeated with a dip of his head.

He picked up his cap from where he'd dropped it and settled it on his head, then turned on the scuffed heel of his boot and headed for the door. He stopped with his hand on the latch.

"Still locked, sir." Was that a hint of laughter in the man's voice? Gerard would love to hear him break loose in a hearty belly laugh. Maybe sometime before he left the abbey, he could make that happen.

"Right." Gerard brushed past Kenway and fit the key to the lock. The fine hairs on the back of his neck rose at the nearness of that large, warm body. One encounter was not nearly enough. He couldn't allow all that raw energy and passion to slip through his fingers, but neither could he demand sexual gratification from an unwilling employee. What to do? He'd simply have to entice Kenway to long for a repeat performance as much as he did.

As the bailiff started through the door, Gerard said, "Tonight, then. I shall look forward to hearing your ideas." And if hearing turned into looking, touching and tasting, he'd make certain it was by Kenway's choice.

Gerard went to find Mrs. Billings to tell her he wouldn't require lunch as he intended to go into the village. A sandwich at the local pub would do him well. He heard the housekeeper before he saw her, her strident voice haranguing one of the under servants, no doubt. What a shock when he rounded the corner and found Mrs. Billings and his own dear valet, Farley, arguing in the hallway.

"I shall see to Mr. Gerard's boots as I've always done. I

don't require anyone else to black them," Farley said.

"I assure you, my staff may be small in number, but we can meet the master's standards," Mrs. Billings replied stiffly. "I'll have Joey see to it."

Gerard noted the aggressive stance of Billings and Farley, facing one another like opposing generals meeting on a battlefield, and recognized it was not the mundane matter of his boots that spurred them to combat. Both were the heads of their respective households, and this was a standoff over whose authority was greater.

Or was it? He observed the way rotund Farley leaned toward plump Mrs. Billings and how the housekeeper's fingers worried at her top dress button below her starched collar. Perhaps there was something else going on here, an attraction that manifested in squabbling. He of all people understood how akin fighting was to lovemaking. Farley, the old dog. Gerard never would have guessed he had it in him.

Gerard retreated before the quarreling servants were even aware of him. Leave them to their aggressive courtship, if that's what it was.

As he headed toward his room, he thought about attraction, lust and that ephemeral thing called love. How strange the feelings that could whip into an unexpected life inside a person at the oddest provocation. What caused one particular person to appear more attractive than all others? What intense passion caused a woman like his mother, for example, to throw away her family for love of an unstable madman? One could never really understand the cravings that drove people's actions.

A quick wash up and change of clothing and Gerard was ready to walk to the village. He found a maid in the hallway to deliver his message about lunch for Mrs. Billings, then set off.

The day had turned a bit overcast and a strong wind blew him along the country road, wrapping his coat around his legs. He looked across the landscape, which appeared less desolate than he'd thought yesterday. Certainly there were empty, wide-open spaces, but there were also quaint cottages and outbuildings to break up the monotony. Sheep dotted a meadow and broom covered a field in blue. It wasn't the dark gray place of his memory but a verdant countryside even under cloudy skies.

About a quarter mile on, Gerard noticed that he had a small shadow keeping pace with him. He glanced back at Ipsial walking along the top of the low stone wall that bordered the road, arms outstretched. The little fellow didn't jump down and hide behind the wall as Gerard half expected but stared cheekily back at him.

"Are you coming to town with me?" Gerard asked. He recalled Kenway's instructions for the boy to meet him by the stable clock. "I believe you have time before Mr. Kenway requires you." So little time had passed for the world to have changed so.

The boy shrugged and leaped over a crumbled gap in the wall.

"If I'm not mistaken, there are jars of candy at the village shop. Perhaps we might stop there and see what they have to offer."

Ipsial jumped down off the wall and crept closer to Gerard. Ah, the power of sweets to create a friendly bond. Now the boy walked nearly by his side, trotting a little to keep up before stopping to kick a stone with the toe of one badly worn boot.

"We should buy you a new pair of shoes," Gerard remarked.

Ipsial said nothing, just kicked the stone again.

"So, you traveled here all by yourself from Cambridge? How

did you get here?"

There was a long silence, and he thought Ipsial might not answer.

"My mum give me money for the train ticket. Then I walked."

Gerard considered a nine-year-old child with the presence of mind to transport himself over one hundred miles all alone. He surmised that Ipsial had been fending for himself for a very long time, and that thought made him feel a rush of protectiveness toward the poor unwanted bastard.

"Well, I'm very glad you came, and I hope you'll be willing to move from the gardener's cottage into the house. I'll have a room prepared for you, whichever one you like."

Ipsial cocked his head.

"What's your favorite color?" Gerard fished for anything to get the boy talking.

"Dunno."

Did the child even know the names of colors? Gerard wouldn't have been surprised at any extent of ignorance. "Do you like this shade of blue?" He indicated his navy coat.

Ipsial shrugged. "I like that." He pointed to the dark maroon scarf Gerard wore around his neck.

"Then you shall have it." Gerard took off the scarf and leaned to wrap it around the boy's neck. Immediately, Ipsial stepped back, so Gerard continued to hold the scarf until he snatched it.

"What color would you say that is? More red or purple?" Gerard tested the boy.

Ipsial stared at him as he wound the scarf around his neck, the fine silk an odd contrast with his patched coat. "It's red, o'course."

"Oh yes, of course it is."

Gerard kept up this inane and mostly one-sided chatter all the way to the village. It was exhausting to entertain a child. But he could almost see Ipsial slowly relaxing. The boy only started to appear nervous again when they neared the cluster of buildings that composed Hedgefield. He walked more slowly.

"It's all right, Ipsial. No one will harm you while you're with me." He debated reaching out and taking the boy by the hand, but that seemed akin to grabbing the paw of a wild creature who'd just as likely bite him as accept the comfort.

Ipsial drew even closer to his side as Gerard led the way down High Street and into the village shop Mrs. Billings had called Greenwood's.

"Good day," he greeted the shopkeeper. "I'm in need of new clothing and footwear for my ward here. Would you have such items available?"

"And sweets," Ipsial reminded him.

"Yes, Mr. Gerard." The thin man studied the pair of them through thick spectacles, probably taking notes to share with the other locals later. "It's good to have you back, sir."

Considering he'd about been the age of Ipsial when he left, Gerard wondered how the man even knew who he was. But then he realized how swiftly news traveled in rural villages. "I thought it was time I saw to my family's estate. I thought Greenwood's was a greengrocers?"

Light glinted off glass lenses as the man studied Ipsial, marking the family resemblance. "I'm Barry Greenwood, sir. My father was the greengrocer, and now my brother runs the business. Tell me what all you need for the boy, and if I don't have it ready-made, my daughter will sew something. She's an able seamstress."

Greenwood located a few premade shirts, trousers and

106

jackets for Ipsial. Gerard tried to convince the boy that he needed to change into them so the seamstress daughter could tailor them to fit. That proved impossible, so he purchased the lot without alteration and ordered them to be sent to the abbey. If the clothes were too large for Ipsial, at least they'd be clean and new. Now if he could only get the boy into a bathtub to wash off the stink before he dressed in his new finery.

Shoes were one thing Ipsial was willing to try on, and soon he was happily clomping around the store in a pair of black calf-high boots with shiny leather toes. He seemed fascinated by their shine and kept stooping over to rub the toes clean.

Their last stop was to examine the confections lined up in jars on the counter. Ipsial wanted to carry the small sack of treats, but Gerard insisted he would dole them out. He'd withhold the rest for future bribes. He allowed Ipsial to jam only a few candies into his jacket pockets and mouth.

After thanking Greenwood for his help and heading back onto the street, Gerard turned to Ipsial. "Are you hungry? I thought we might go to the public house."

Heaven knew it had been a long time since breakfast, with much activity to work up an appetite. And, oh, how the memory of some of those activities made him want to go rushing back to the abbey for a repeat performance.

"A'right," Ipsial mumbled around a mouthful of toffee.

While the boy now seemed more relaxed about their visit to the village, Gerard's tension built as he led the way to the Goat and Grape. There would be plenty of looks and whispered conversations concerning his reappearance after so many years away—and about the paternity of Ipsial. He'd rather have gone home and avoided the gossip but reminded himself he was here for a reason—to check the temperature of the locals and see where his family stood with them.

The great room of the tavern was dark and smelled of years of spilled ale and tobacco smoke. Heads swiveled toward the newcomers, and once more Ipsial pressed quite close to Gerard's side. This time he dared rest a steadying hand on the boy's shoulder while steering him toward a table, and, wonder of wonders, his hand wasn't bitten.

Gerard ordered sandwiches, and soon Ipsial was devouring thick slabs of meat in bread. Food distracted him from the watchful eyes, but Gerard was well aware of them. He felt he should somehow introduce himself to the community and make friendly chitchat with these people, but there seemed to be no natural way to join in on the private conversations going on at other tables.

Then one brave soul ventured over to the table to say hello, a portly gray-haired fellow.

"Good day, Mr. Gerard. My name is Burton Reynolds. My son-in-law, John White, is the proprietor of this establishment. Speaking on behalf of everyone in the village, I'd like to welcome you home."

"Thank you, Mr. Reynolds."

"Are you here to stay, then?" Mr. Reynolds looked between him and Ipsial and raised his eyebrows expectantly.

Gerard had no interest in discussing his plans or ideas of his future with a man he didn't know, especially since he didn't know what his plans were yet. Ipsial seemed involved with a bit of sticky candy he held in his hand, but he might well be listening.

Gerard had long ago learned how to be politely evasive. He said, "It's good to be here. My recollections of the area are foggy, but it seems quite built up and improved."

The old man beamed at him as if he'd just announced the village had won the prize as the prettiest in England. "Yes,

108

indeed, sir." He examined Ipsial with bright, interested eyes from under the shaggy eyebrows. "And I believe this lad lives up at the abbey as well? Are you a good boy, then?"

"Huh." Ipsial poked at the damp candy he cupped on his palm before popping it back into his mouth. He made a face at Mr. Reynolds that could have been a jeer or perhaps resulted from his jaws working the candy.

Gerard wanted to tell the child to mind his manners, to say hello when he'd been spoken to, but they were a long way from that sort of admonition—and he had no right. And there was the fact that he had no notion what the untamed Ipsial might do or say if rebuked. So Gerard stayed mute and watched with amusement and dread.

Mr. Reynolds leaned forward over his considerable belly to rest his hands on his knees. "I have a question for you, boy. Might you know about some missing chickens?"

"Chickens?" Ipsial raised his head at last. "What 'ud I do with them?" His scorn was obvious.

"Some housewives have reported that several fowl have gone missing in the village. And other things as well." He glanced up at Gerard and gave an apologetic duck of the head. "Before you come back, sir."

"Mister here don't know about nothing," Ipsial said. Was it a way to grant Gerard an excuse from any illegal activities or to point out he was a dunce?

"Ipsial. Have you stolen anything from the village?" Gerard asked gently.

"Huh." That grunt seemed to be his all-purpose answer for difficult questions. "No, 'course not," he added a moment later, not very convincingly. Gerard supposed that the silver lining to the cloud of Ipsial's life of crime was that the boy was apparently not a good liar.

Mr. Reynolds eyed Ipsial, then examined Gerard's face for a moment before returning his obviously fascinated gaze to the boy. Gerard could only guess what sort of stories the old man might be creating to tell villagers who visited the inn.

Mr. Reynolds straightened his bulk and pointed at Gerard's tumbler that had held a measure of homebrew. "May I buy you a refill, sir?"

"No, no, thank you, Mr. Reynolds. We must return to the abbey." He rose to his feet.

"Right." Ipsial sniffed and muttered something that might have been, "Mr. Kenway's gonna give me hell."

Gerard made a halfhearted effort to remedy the mistake of coming here. "But, Mr. Reynolds, pray allow me to buy one for you." Gerard approached the barmaid and held out some coins. "A drink for every man in the place, if you please."

"Thank you, sir," someone called, and a gruff "Thank'ee" from everyone in the room followed.

Gerard returned to the bench where they'd sat. He grabbed his packages and nodded in acknowledgement to the thanks. "I am glad to be back," he said. "Thank you for the welcome, Mr. Reynolds. Ipsial, come."

He walked away quickly, hoping Ipsial would follow.

At the end of the High Street, Gerard slowed a little when he heard feet thumping after him. Ipsial appeared at his side, and they walked out of the village together, in surprisingly companionable silence.

Ipsial was absorbed in watching his own feet. "First new ones I had," he said at last with awe.

As he and Ipsial walked over a small rise, Gerard was surprised by how the sight of the abbey on the hill no longer filled him with dread. Indeed, he now felt a surge of anticipation for the coming evening. Miles Kenway would come to him and then... He found his body tensing and his cock swelling slightly in expectation.

He shook off the excitement and walked faster until he grew almost out of breath. Ipsial scampered to catch up.

Gerard asked, "So, do you wish to move your things to the big house?"

A frown creased the boy's forehead as he scuffed his shiny new shoes in the dirt. He shook his head and, quick as a deer, veered off the road and leaped onto the bordering stone wall. He gave Gerard one backward glance before dropping on the other side.

Gerard stared after him. "Well, all right, then." Just as well, since he wasn't up to the task of seeing the boy was bathed before dressing in his new clothes. Tomorrow would be soon enough to tackle that project, he hoped with the help of Mrs. Billings or perhaps Kenway.

He increased his pace, hurrying with his packages toward the dark shape of the sprawling building silhouetted by the setting sun. A sense of coming home was the last thing he'd ever expected to feel about this place. Again, what a difference a day made—and the promise of another encounter with the surprising Mr. Kenway.

Chapter Eleven

Miles wound the stable yard clock as he did every other day, then climbed down from the wooden box and put it in the empty stable. The boy was a few minutes late. Kenway was about to give up when Ipsial appeared in the yard.

"Why are you barefoot?"

The boy owned a pair of ragged boots with holes, but at least they kept his feet slightly protected.

"Mister threw 'em away."

"Mr. Gerard? Threw away your shoes?"

Ipsial nodded. "Got me some new ones."

"Why aren't you wearing them?"

Ipsial gave him a look of pure scorn. "What, and get them dirty?"

Miles folded his arms. "Go fetch them. We are going to make a fire, and you'll need shoes to protect your feet."

Ipsial's eyes widened. "A fire? A big one?"

"Yes. A bonfire. But not unless you get your new shoes."

"Boots," Ipsial corrected, then disappeared. Miles sighed.

He'd wait another fifteen minutes and then get to work whether or not the boy reappeared. He had planned to make a waste fire later in the month, but a bonfire seemed the ideal answer for Ipsial. The boy would have to work, yet gain some reward because he probably enjoyed a crackling fire as much as the next child. Of course, because this was Ipsial, Miles might be teaching him to be an arsonist. At least he was keeping the boy away from firearms, and that was a happy change.

In less than five minutes, Ipsial reappeared, and the two of them toiled, dragging fallen tree limbs into a clearing not far from the old monks' burial ground.

The fire started easily enough with the brush Miles had already placed in the circle of rocks set there for the purpose. Now they dumped dry leaves and other garden waste on the fire. Miles was pleased to see that Ipsial could work hard. The boy's eyes went wide when Miles produced a couple of potatoes he'd dug from his kitchen garden and showed Ipsial how to push them into the coals to cook.

When something in the fire popped, Ipsial jumped and dove to the ground.

"It's all right," Miles said. "Just the sap in a green branch."

Ipsial, who'd been almost pleasant company for almost an hour, sneered. "I know that." Miles watched him and saw that his hands trembled. Interesting how he was like Gerard. Fear made him angry.

Gerard. The thought reminded him that he was to meet the man again today. Miles must get ready. He stopped Ipsial from dragging another branch to the fire. "We will allow it to die back. You have been a champion helper, and I can take care of the rest."

"What about the potatoes?"

Miles grabbed a stick and dug them out. He found a rag at the edge of the fire and wrapped it around the potatoes.

For the first time, Ipsial didn't run away as soon as he got what he wanted. He sat by the fire, poking the potatoes with twigs while they cooled.

"Did you enjoy your visit to the village?" Miles asked.

Ipsial nodded and actually turned his pale peaky face to

look at him. "I guess I didn't steal any chickens."

Miles had no idea what he meant but said, "No? Good for you."

Ipsial nodded, more definitely now. He touched a potato and drew back a finger quickly.

"Are you hungry?" Miles pulled the end of a loaf of bread from his other pocket and tossed it to Ipsial, whose hand shot out and snapped it like dog.

But he held up the bread and examined it rather than shoving it into his mouth. "I'm eating so much today I'll explode. Like sap." The boy actually grinned at Miles.

A shared joke?

Miles felt as if he'd just been given a valuable gift. "Disgusting," he said cheerfully. "Your insides will be strewn every which way."

Ipsial snickered, and at the sheer pleasure of the sound, Miles joined him in laughter.

Gerard dressed for dinner but ate with little appetite. Alone at the large table in the dimly lit room, he remembered again how shadowy and eerie this house was. He missed his London home, or, better yet, the house he'd taken in southern Italy last winter. The light, colors and scents of that cottage on the beautiful Mediterranean enticed him to spend another dismal English winter abroad. Perhaps after he'd got things settled here, he'd take another trip. But at present, Italy and the future were a world away. He had more immediate pleasures to consider.

He pushed away his plate and went to the study for an after-dinner smoke. The draw of tobacco in his lungs and a sip of heady cognac blurred the keen edge of his excitement. Still, he found it impossible to relax in his father's chair. Unfortunately, he hadn't been precise in setting a time.

For that matter, he didn't know if the bailiff would show at all. Kenway had seemed shaken by their encounter in the billiard room and determined not to repeat it. He might choose to stay away from his randy employer rather than risk another session.

No. Gerard's desires clamored for more. He couldn't bear the thought of not exploring the possibilities with Kenway further. Damn, he was more entranced by this unsophisticated man than he'd ever been by the dandies he'd met on his travels.

A cigar and two drinks later, Gerard was getting more agitated and annoyed. He paced the length of the study, pausing to stare out the windows at blackness, and had just come to the conclusion that if the mountain wouldn't come to Mohammed...when there was a light rap at the door.

He hurried to sit and assume a casual pose staring into the fireplace before calling, "Come in."

Kenway strode through the doorway, along with a burst of fresh outdoor air. He must have been burning brush or leaves, because he smelled deliciously of wood smoke. Gerard wanted to leap up and tear off his coat, strip him completely naked and run his hands over smooth skin rather than rough wool.

"Do come in. Sit," he ordered calmly despite his pounding pulse.

Kenway took the armchair across from his and lowered his oversized frame into it. His gaze didn't quite meet Gerard's. He thrust a sheaf of papers toward him.

"So, this is the list of my suggestions to improve the abbey, ordered from most imperative to least," he said briskly. "The roof cannot wait, sir."

"Very good." Gerard reached for the papers, and Kenway let go before he'd gotten hold of them. Several fluttered to the carpet. Both men bent to get them, and their heads cracked together.

Kenway cursed, and Gerard laughed and rubbed his noggin. "Please, Kenway, try to control your enthusiasm for the project. There will be plenty of time to go over all your plans. For now, can't we sit and enjoy one another's company?"

Kenway sat back, rubbing his forehead. "I don't know if that's wise, sir. If you're not ready to discuss the abbey, then I think I should probably leave."

He made no sign of rising from his seat.

"Or you could have a drink of this excellent brandy I found." Setting the list of home improvements aside, Gerard reached for the decanter. "God knows how long it's been sitting here, gathering dust. I have no idea when my father last visited the abbey."

Kenway accepted the glass and didn't drop it when his fingers brushed against Gerard's. "Might I ask, sir, what event caused your family to abandon the property?"

Gerard was taken aback. The bailiff went from subservient to inappropriately inquisitive with remarkable speed.

Gerard answered with a version of the truth without revealing the story. "My mother's death," he answered simply. "It shook my father to the core. I don't believe he could bear to come here after that. I certainly couldn't."

"I'm sorry. Losing a parent at any age is difficult, but for one so young..."

So, Kenway knew a bit of his history. Gerard wondered how much. What rumors from the village had filled his ears?

"Anyway, I'd prefer not to discuss my past," Gerard

interrupted.

"Nor do you want to discuss the estate repairs. So what *do* you want, sir?"

Gerard simply stared back at him, leaving the obvious answer hanging unspoken in the air between them. A few moments of quiet broken only by the crackling of the fire on the hearth passed.

"Tell me, Mr. Kenway. How is it that a Yorkshire farmer's son usually speaks with such an educated air?"

Kenway's eyes narrowed slightly. "Books, sir, are for all to read. It doesn't take a Cambridge University education to acquire knowledge."

"Of course." Gerard felt shamed by his supposition that all lower-class men were incapable of aspiring to greater knowledge.

Kenway said, "Ah well, you wouldn't hire a bailiff you thought had no sense or education."

Gerard didn't bother pointing out that he hadn't cared about his family's home when he'd interviewed candidates for the position.

The bailiff sounded much friendlier as he continued, "I've always had a fondness for reading and became an addict during a particularly long Canadian winter. And I've purchased a small collection of my own over the years. I hope you don't mind, sir, but I've used your family's extensive library since I've been here."

"Of course." Hadn't he just said that? Gerard cleared his throat. He had long ago left behind a boy's awkwardness, but this surprising, intriguing man occasionally sent him straight back to those uncomfortable years. The bailiff's physical presence made him achingly aware of his own body, Kenway's body, and what they might do together. Now Kenway's words

117

forced him to pay heed to his mind as well.

He gripped the arms of his chair and forced himself to calm. Kenway seemed to require conversation. He groped for a topic that would not send either of them flying into a state. "Did young Ipsial appear at his appointed time?"

Kenway also seemed to relax at the question. "Indeed, sir. He showed up barefoot and informed me that you'd tossed his shoes in the waste bin."

"What?" Gerard gave a startled laugh.

"Don't worry, sir. I made him retrieve his new boots." Kenway described the bonfire he and the boy made.

"Your plan sounds ideal, except of course, if the young blighter decides to set the gardener's cottage on fire."

"Precisely my own worry. I might have made it clear that if I caught him playing with fire, he'd be in serious trouble."

"Much good that will do," Gerard said. Kenway smiled at him, and they were in perfect accord.

"Do you think it will be possible to train him?" Gerard asked. "Can he be civilized?"

Kenway rose to his feet. He stared into the fire, which danced over his golden skin and lit his eyes. "I am determined, sir." He hesitated, then continued, "Sometime this afternoon I felt as if we, Ipsial and I, had a connection that meant I could not ignore him even if I wished to."

Gerard recalled the walk into the village and the moment that he too felt the surge of protective instinct for the boy. "Yes, and I shall lend aid, of course. Your sister? Have you written to her?"

"Should I, sir? Have you decided on that?" He sounded slightly sharp.

Perhaps because it had been another topic Gerard had

sloughed off in his hurry to get his hands on Kenway. He rubbed his palms together now to thwart that eagerness.

"Indeed I have decided. Please write to her. Do you know which cottage she might occupy?"

"Wouldn't she stay with me?"

"You don't have enough room for her and her two children."

And if she lived with Kenway, it would be difficult for him to escape to the abbey proper. He inhaled sharply at the thought of Kenway, late at night slipping into his room, walking into his arms.

Except the man in question didn't move from his place by the fire or look around. He said, "My house here is almost as large as the home we occupied as children."

Gerard dragged himself from the imaginings of stripping the clothes from his bailiff. "Bah. There is a perfectly good cottage on the far side of the burial ground. Rose Cottage, I think it's called?"

"It requires rethatching and other repairs."

"Very well. Put that at the top of your list." He touched the sheaves of paper. "And of course the slate roof over the main hall."

"Yes. I am glad the library is safe now. And the rest of it, sir?"

"Two jobs at a time, Kenway." He did not want to peruse the list. No, he wanted to study that blunt no-nonsense nose, those full, chapped lips.

Kenway twisted on his heel, a dark scowl on his hard face. "You didn't summon me here to discuss the work I do. Tell me. What do you want from me?"

Gerard wouldn't move. "Are you the sort who likes to hear his partner in crime beg?"

"Crime, sir?"

"Is that what you truly believe? That pleasure should be prosecuted as a criminal act?"

Kenway frowned but then shook his head. "No. When I have thought of this... No."

Gerard felt a surge of glee but hid it as he glanced around the dark paneled study, with its red carpet and the arching windows that echoed the original abbey's shapes. "This is a comfortable room, don't you think?"

"Mr. Gerard—"

"Just Gerard. My friends call me that."

"No one calls you Everett?"

"No. Never." He didn't want to get into the matter of his cousin Hubert and the awful nickname. He rose from the chair and walked to stand next to Kenway.

He would not be the one to give in first. Though his mouth went dry with desire, he would not touch Kenway. The larger man's chest rose and fell in uneven breaths. "Yes," he said.

Was that an invitation? Gerard asked, "Yes, what?"

"The room. It...it's comfortable." He looked at something over Gerard's shoulder. Gerard turned to see Kenway's attention was on the carved settee with the velvet cushion.

"That doesn't look particularly comfortable, does it? I'd say the floor offered more comfort. Or perhaps the *causeuse*?" He waved a hand at the round sofa in the middle of the room.

Kenway's fleeting smile seemed nervous. "That what those round things are called? German is it?"

"That is simply French for sofa. But it does offer interesting ideas, doesn't it?" The sofa in question was uglier than sin, with a hump rising from its center and elaborate tassels encircling the bottom.

Kenway's full lips moved, then went tight. "Yes," he said again.

"And this yes means...?"

"The ideas. Yes, it offers ideas." Kenway twisted to face Gerard, whose heart began to thump so hard he raised his hand to his own chest.

They stood so close together his knuckles grazed Kenway's rough wool waistcoat, and he could hear the other man's labored breathing—not from any physical strain but from the heat growing between them. The scent of wood smoke emanated from Kenway, and somehow, in Gerard's mind, he equated it with the conflagration which was about to consume them. But at Kenway's command—only at his command.

Gerard waited.

"Damnation." Kenway growled.

Suddenly his long arms were wrapped around Gerard and pulling him close. His rough mouth savaged Gerard's with hard, insistent kisses that made Gerard gulp in surprise. "Umph."

Kenway pulled back and stared into his face with darkly dilated eyes. "This is what you wanted, isn't it? It's why you invited me here to 'discuss improvements'."

"Yes." Gerard hugged that big body up hard against his own. "I know I promised to leave it, but I don't want to. I want more of you, Miles Kenway. And I believe you want more of me."

Kenway didn't deny it. Instead, he returned to kissing Gerard as if his mouth were a lifeline keeping the man afloat—desperate, greedy kisses that drove all thoughts out of Gerard's mind, leaving only sensation. Jesus, none of his continental paramours had kissed like this. They had more finesse, more sinuous expertise with their tongues, but they'd lacked the sheer *hunger* that Kenway exhibited; they hadn't given him the feeling that he was necessary to their very survival.

Gerard let go of Kenway long enough to push the coat off his shoulders. He pressed Kenway's lips with another kiss while his fingers fumbled the buttons of his waistcoat. God, he was actually shaking with need and excitement as he worked to strip the other man down to his skin.

Kenway seized his arms and pushed him roughly away, and Gerard let out a surprised grunt of disappointment. But Kenway only said, "The door. You never locked it."

"Right. Yes." The likelihood of Mrs. Billings or any other servant coming in the study was small, but it was, of course, better not to take any chances. He rushed over to the door, catching his toe on a worn spot in the carpet and tripping before he reached it. Gerard laughed at his own reckless enthusiasm. It was as if he'd never done this before. He felt young and giddy and new.

He managed to get the key turned in the lock and turned to find Kenway half naked, stripped down to his trousers and rapidly divesting himself of those. Gerard felt a moment of shock at the sight of that large, hard-muscled body, the dark hair on Kenway's chest, and the brown nipples that stood in sharp relief against his pale skin. Somehow he'd expected Kenway would act more the blushing virgin, forcing Gerard to take control and strip him down. But Kenway appeared surprisingly eager and uninhibited as he pulled off his boots and let his trousers drop to the floor, making Gerard wonder exactly how much experience the man had had.

What a fine specimen of a man. Gerard decided there was no harm in letting Kenway know that. "What a fine specimen you are." He repeated the thought aloud.

Kenway didn't respond, perhaps embarrassed by the compliment. Rather, he finished removing his drawers and stood, hands lightly clenched at his sides, gazing at Gerard with a "now what?" expression on his face.

Gerard sauntered over with more casualness than he felt. He studied the thick erection thrusting from a dark brown thatch of hair. He stood fully clothed before Kenway and reached out to encircle the throbbing cock in his hand. He could feel the lifeblood pulsing through it, warming his palm.

"Lovely man, what shall I do with you? Would you like me to...?" He lowered himself to his knees, gaze lifted to meet Kenway's, and brought the damp tip of that cock to his mouth.

One lick across the head and then he engulfed it, sucking the relentless length deep into his throat until he nearly choked.

Kenway whimpered, and his hips rocked in response. For several moments, Gerard allowed the other man to fuck his mouth at will; then he pulled off and sat back on his heels.

"Like that? Is that what you long for?"

"Yes," Kenway hissed and clasped Gerard's head between his big hands to guide him back toward his twitching cock.

"Tsk," Gerard berated him. "You must learn to ask nicely for what you crave. Say 'please'."

"Please," Kenway gritted between teeth.

"Please what? Tell me. Say you want me to suck you." Gerard caught his breath, excited almost beyond endurance at the thought of hearing this calm, self-possessed man beg for sex.

Kenway glared down at him, eyes narrowed, but he seemed to understand the game they were playing. "Please...sir," he said. "Please won't you suck my cock?"

The hot words dropped like candle wax on his skin, burning sweet, fiery trails all through him. Gerard bent to his task, taking Kenway's erection in hand again and swallowing it deeply. He bobbed his head up and down, willingly gagging himself in an effort to engulf as much of Kenway's flesh as possible. He listened to Kenway's rapid breathing and soft groans and judged carefully when the man was reaching his peak. Only then did he encircle the base of Kenway's cock with his fingers and squeeze to stop him from coming too soon.

"Wait," Gerard urged as he scrambled to his feet.

"I don't want to wait." Kenway's gruff voice sent shivers through him. "I want you now."

And then he was tearing off Gerard's clothing with such haste that buttons flew and cloth ripped. Gerard helped, loosening his tie and toeing off shoes, until he was stripped naked. He lunged at Kenway, wrapping his arms around that hard body and feeling the weight and warmth of muscles and cock pressed against him.

Gerard was flexible about lovemaking. He would take the bottom or the top, depending on the lover he was with. Right now, it seemed clear that Kenway wanted to fuck him rather than be fucked, and Gerard was happy to oblige. His anus clenched in anticipation of being filled.

For a few moments, they kissed and clutched every available inch of flesh, and then Kenway abruptly flung Gerard away from him—right onto the cushioned round sofa. It was harder than any piece of furniture had a right to be, stuffed with horsehair or perhaps sawdust, and that hump in the middle hit him in the chest. But Gerard happily maintained his pose—draped over the *causeuse*, limbs sprawled and arse lifted invitingly.

He glanced at Kenway over his shoulder, feeling a bit smug about the smoldering desire in the man's eyes as his gaze raked over Gerard's body.

"There's a jar of ointment there on the table," Gerard

suggested.

A smile flitted over Kenway's mouth. "Still insisting you called me here to discuss the abbey? Your preparation suggests otherwise."

Gerard watched the man pick up the jar from the table, study the label, then glance over at Gerard's nude arse. It was easy to guess this was the first time Miles Kenway had done this, and the idea that it was all brand-new to him increased Gerard's excitement, making him feel as if it were his first time again too.

"You can smear that on your prick to ease your passage."

"I know that," Kenway said with the injured air of a man whose prowess has been doubted. "I know what I'm doing. What we're doing."

Gerard fell silent then and waited, anticipating the first touch of Kenway's fingers to his rear. He closed his eyes and sighed as a callused palm stroked down his spine and cupped his backside, and he moaned a little when a finger slid between his cheeks and intruded on his most private spot. He tensed slightly, and his muscles clenched around Kenway's probing finger. To demonstrate his acceptance, he rocked back, forcing Kenway to push deeper.

Seconds later, the thick, blunt finger was replaced by a much thicker knob. Kenway's hairy thighs pressed against his arse as he eased his length inside Gerard. His body stretched around Kenway's cock, and Gerard listened for the man's response to this strange new sensation. He was rewarded with a quiet gulp as Kenway swallowed.

Gerard adored the sound of a lover's voice, and he particularly wanted to hear Kenway's gruff need. "Do you like how I feel around you? Tell me what it's like."

"Shh," Kenway said, curving his heavy body over Gerard's

back and cupping the back of his neck in one palm. The commanding, controlling weight of him silenced Gerard. Not everyone was as verbal as he chose to be during sex. He'd entice more words out of Miles another time.

Miles. How odd to think of the man by his given name rather than as Kenway the bailiff. And yet it felt natural, a comfortable, informal address. Although he could never call him by name in public, in the secret moments they shared, or at least in his mind, Gerard would refer to him as Miles from now on.

Gerard relaxed his muscles to allow Miles's cock to slide more easily inside. The familiar burn and stretch and the solid length of the other man probing deeper still filled his senses. Muscle and bone, heat and damp flesh wrestling together—not so very different from fisticuffs after all. Pinned beneath the other man's weight, Gerard submitted utterly. Minor annoyances such as the stiff damask scratching his skin or the hard sofa pressing into his chest only enhanced the experience. Gerard had learned that discomfort or pain made one's senses more acute so he could more fully experience pleasure as well. And, oh, there was *great* pleasure in Miles's cock drilling, filling, willing him to surrender.

Gerard could hold back no longer. "Ah yes," he crooned when Miles hit a certain spot inside him. "Right there. Please. Please. Deeper. Harder. Make it hurt."

Miles obliged. Spurred by the breathless commands, he thrust harder and faster, his groin slapping loudly against Gerard's arse. Gerard gripped the slippery fabric of the sofa and dug his bare feet more firmly into the carpet to brace his body against the onslaught. Miles was frantic, thrusting erratically, losing control and ramming into Gerard like a man possessed. The burning sensation was heavenly.

After several moments, Miles groaned low in his throat and his body shuddered. So quickly? How long had the poor man held back all the desperate need inside him? His entire life, Gerard guessed. And now it came out in one powerful surge. Gerard pushed back against the powerful thigh muscles pinning him to the sofa and accepted every drop Miles had to offer.

"Good," he whispered. "So good. Give it all to me."

Christ, was that a sob that tore from the other man's throat? Gerard's eyes flew open, but in his field of vision was only the overstuffed furniture, books piled on a table and an ugly hunting painting on one wall. How he longed to see Miles's face right now. It would be astounding to witness. But perhaps another time.

For the present, Gerard remained very still beneath the weight collapsed on top of him. He would not say a word or make a move to end Miles's prolonged moment of bliss. Nor would he ever mention the quiet sob he was quite certain he'd heard. Even between lovers there was separation, wells of reserve, walls behind which hidden feelings remained. Miles's intense emotion was his own to savor.

When at last Miles pulled away, withdrawing his depleted cock and removing his weight and hot flesh, Gerard drew a deep breath into his constricted lungs. He pushed himself up and turned to sit on the sofa.

Miles stood before him, breathing heavily, hair rumpled and body shining with sweat.

"Have you been satisfied?" Gerard asked.

"Yes, sir. Quite satisfied." A rumor of a smile curved Miles's mouth.

"Very good." Gerard smiled back. Beneath him, he felt a warm trickle and imagined a wet stain was spotting the damask; the residue of sex, so basic and foreign to this stuffy room. He quite liked the idea of leaving a mark of life behind in this dead edifice.

"But you haven't been," Miles said. "Satisfied, I mean. Let me..." He started to go to his knees before Gerard, and truly Gerard wouldn't at all have minded that luscious mouth on his cock, but he reached for the bailiff. "Wait. Sit beside me here on this most uncomfortable piece of furniture."

Miles obliged, awkwardly fitting himself onto the circular seat beside Gerard. Thighs pressed together, they sat, and Gerard snaked an arm around Miles's back. He leaned to press a kiss to his still-heaving chest.

"Don't you want me to finish you?" Miles frowned at Gerard's swollen cock.

In answer, Gerard took Miles's hand and molded it around him. "Like this will be fine," he said, then cupped the other man's jaw and brought their mouths together. He kissed those weathered lips and tasted the salt of sweat and the peaty flavor of wood smoke.

Miles took his cue, returning the kiss with a deep, almost reverent attention, while briskly massaging Gerard's erection.

He was so close to the edge that each pull of that rough fist was like sandpaper scraping him and added to the growing ache. But, oh, such a *good* ache that it made him whimper for more. Gerard latched on to Miles's mouth and swirled his tongue around the other man's, and his hips rocked as he thrust himself into Miles's hand. *There. There. And right...now!*

His pleasure squirted out in white spurts over the fist that held him so tight. Gerard broke off the kiss to gasp for air, and he lost all sense of place or time as waves of delight swept through him.

After a moment, his eyes flickered open and focused on

Miles again. Blue eyes stared back at him, watching him, taking the image and filing it away in memory. And Gerard understood that this was no mere diversion for a man like Miles Kenway. He was apparently a restless man, unable or uninterested in settling in one place for long, yet the solid, dependable Kenway did not seem the capricious sort in other matters. Gerard may have plunged into this on a whim, but for Miles to engage in acts of perversion with his employer *meant* something. And that was quite a frightful thought, so with typical nonchalance, Gerard broke off the somber moment.

"Here, let me get you something." He disentangled his arms from around Miles and dove for his jacket on the floor, from the pocket of which he withdrew a handkerchief. He handed it to Miles and watched him wipe the residue from his hand.

Now what? Always the question after a sexual encounter. If Gerard were with his friends on the continent—someone like the conte—he would suggest a stroll to a nearby café for pastries or a walk through some ancient ruins, but here and with this man, what was there to say or do?

Could they discuss art or books? He had already insulted Miles's cultural education. Someday soon he'd venture into such topics and learn what the intriguing Mr. Kenway thought when he looked at a painting or read a novel. But now, while they were still near-strangers, it might be perceived as an attempt to show superiority.

He realized he wanted more than these so very lively interactions. He wished to know the man better.

"Well, then..." His brain was a blank canvas. Not a thought inhabited it. And then a light flickered. "Ipsial. I need to coerce the boy into a bath tomorrow, and then I hope to convince him to move his things into a room in the house. Don't suppose you have any idea how to accomplish those two goals?"

"Bribery seems to have served you quite well," Miles said. "But if all else fails, perhaps he could be strong-armed into the tub, ensuring he has a healthy terror of water for the rest of his life."

Gerard laughed. "Ah yes. The traumas of our youth do linger, don't they?"

Miles opened his mouth, appeared about to say something, then closed it again. He rose from the *causeuse* and bent to gather his clothing. Gerard felt a silly stab of disappointment that he was preparing to leave. How nice it would be to retire to bed together, but of course, that couldn't be.

Both men dressed. Miles finished first, and as he snugged his cap on his head, he said, "I expect I'll see you tomorrow then, sir."

"Yes. I expect you shall." Gerard realized he was grinning like a fool and struggled to maintain some semblance of casual dispassion. "Good evening, then."

But the moment the door closed behind the bailiff, his smile broke free again.

Chapter Twelve

"Heaven knows I would like to oblige, sir." Mrs. Billings was at her very stiffest. "But the young man will not undress himself, and I do not have the strength to force him to disrobe. I have requested aid from your manservant, Mr. Farley, but he stated that he would not bathe any unwilling subject."

Gerard hid the smile. Mrs. Billings didn't need to see his amusement. He put down his book. "Very well. You have locked the young man in the bathroom?"

"Sir, yes. He is extremely quiet," she added darkly. "In my experience when young people are too quiet, they are plotting mischief. Perhaps we should send word to Mr. Kenway. He has had the most success with the young...man."

Gerard, who'd been trying to relax with a novel and ignore the shouting coming from the upper story, got to his feet. He had *not* been mooning about, thinking of Kenway, and he also refused to pay heed to his suddenly elated mood. "Yes. I recall he offered to help. Send Joey off to find Mr. Kenway."

She gave a dignified nod and strode from the study, the keys at her waist jingling in a determined fashion.

Just a day ago, he'd posed by that fireplace, nervous as a student facing his first examination. He'd be calmer today, though the thought of what they'd done together gave him a shiver of anticipatory pleasure.

But after almost half an hour, when Mrs. Billings didn't reappear, he went in search of her. And when he heard the soft deep voice drifting down the back stairway, he froze.

Of course Mrs. Billings would take care of the situation and not disturb him again. She'd fetch Mr. Kenway to do the work she required, which was not stopping in to visit with the master. He walked up the stairs quietly to investigate.

Miles suspected that Ipsial had a future as a merchant, a politician or an extortionist.

"If I take off this here boot, I get some of that candy from the village. The spicy one," Ipsial declared.

"Both boots." Miles had been in the room for at least ten minutes, and the heat had long since forced him to remove his jacket and roll up his sleeves.

Ipsial put out his hand.

"I'll give you a horehound drop after both boots come off, and stockings too, if you're wearing them."

The boy carefully unlaced and removed his boots—no socks. An instant later, he held out his hand.

Miles managed to coax and bribe all of the clothes off, except the shabby trousers. He dipped his hands into the water to show how pleasant bathing could be.

Ipsial glared at him. "Not doing this in front of you," he muttered.

Miles's heart sank. He straightened and rubbed his wet hands on one of the towels. Of course the boy would have that fear after witnessing the kiss between him and Gerard—and Miles was *not* dwelling on that kiss right now.

"Ipsial," he said firmly. "You have nothing to fear from me."

The boy stared back.

"I have no interest in, er, you. None."

"Then why you making me bathe?"

"It's my job. And I actually like you, young fathead. When I say interest, I mean something prurient..." Of course the boy didn't know the word. Miles's face grew warm as he tried to find a way to discuss the matter without sounding disgusting. "I won't do anything to harm you. Understand?"

The boy just looked at him. He'd picked up one of his new boots and clutched it to his pale chest.

"Have I ever hurt you before?" Miles asked, desperate.

"You grabbed my arm." He held out his arm, palm down.

Miles examined the pale skinny limb for signs of a bruise and saw plenty of dirt. "Then I apologize. I was attempting to keep you safe. I swear I shall not hurt you unless I feel you are in danger."

Ipsial sniffed. "What do I put on after?"

"Your new clothes. You heard Mrs. Billings say she has gone to fetch them."

"What if they get dirty?"

"They are fresh and clean." *Unlike you.*

"I mean when I wear them."

"They *will* get dirty, and when they do, they shall be washed."

"I don't want 'em to get dirty."

"If you put them on without washing yourself, they'll be dirtied from the inside out." Miles was tired of negotiating and contemplated picking up the young idiot and dumping him headfirst into the full tub, although that would mean he'd break his word less than a minute after giving it.

They examined the large tub, half full of steaming water and some sort of blue-ish salts that smelled like fruit. A pleasant scent, Miles thought, though not the one he'd smelled on Gerard's skin. He firmly chivvied his thoughts back to the proper path. "If you want your new clothes, you must bathe. Mr. Gerard would agree with me."

Ipsial slowly nodded. "All right. I'll do it myself."

"I will give you ten minutes before I check on your progress. You must wash with soap and rinse yourself. And don't forget to wash your hair." He'd worry about cutting the shaggy mane at some future date. Miles pointed at the towel. "And dry yourself with the towel."

"I know that," Ipsial said with magnificent scorn. A second later he added, "But the towel's clean."

"Yes. And so shall you be in less than ten minutes."

Miles left his jacket draped over the small screen in the corner. He slipped from the steamy room, closed the door behind him, then leaned an ear to the door, listening. A second later, he heard a soft splash, as if a boy had climbed into a tub.

Footsteps sounded behind him. "I think we won this round of the battle, Mrs. Billings," Miles said.

"Do you think so?" came Gerard's amused voice. "Shall we win the war?"

"Sir." Miles straightened. He shoved his hands in his pocket, realized they were still damp from the demonstrations he'd done for Ipsial to show the ease of washing and pulled them back out. *Stop fidgeting,* he ordered himself.

"I thought you were Mrs. Billings with the boy's new clothes."

"She'll return momentarily." He drew closer. "I hope you're well today, Miles?"

"Certainly, sir. Fine." He forced himself to look into his employer's face. Those blue eyes seemed to darken, so intense that Miles had to shift his gaze down to Gerard's mouth and then his broad shoulders.

Miles couldn't draw enough air into his body, couldn't stop himself. Just a small brush of his fingers over Gerard's cheek. No one would know or care. He reached, allowing only fingertips against the smooth-shaved cheek, drawing down to trace the corner of the curving mouth. That smile. Lord, what a smile...

"Oi! Mr. Kenway." The boy's voice was muffled by the door.

Miles blinked. What was he doing? Standing in the hallway outside the bath, touching his employer. He stepped back. "What do you need, Ipsial?" His voice emerged as a croak.

"I'm nearly done. You said more candy."

Miles reached into his trouser pocket for the small sack of treats. But Gerard blocked the door.

"Sir?" Miles asked in a low voice.

Gerard called, "Your clothes aren't ready quite yet, Ipsial. Enjoy yourself a minute or two longer. You'll find it's fun to splash about." With one long stride, he brought his body hard up against Miles and drew him in for a long kiss.

When Gerard let go, he would have moved away, but Miles had wrapped his arms tight around him.

Someone's shoes tapped up the back stairs, and Miles hastily released his grip. He wanted to sprint away. He settled for unrolling his shirtsleeves and hastily pulling at the edges of his waistcoat.

Gerard had the nerve to chuckle.

Mrs. Billings stopped in the hall when she saw Gerard. "Sir, did we disturb you? Has that boy made too much noise?"

"Of course not." Gerard took the clothes from her. "We shall take care of the young...of Ipsial. Thank you, Mrs. Billings."

She gave a stiff little nod and hurried back down the stairs.

"The servants here treat me as if I'm liable to have a fit if crossed or disturbed." He turned and scowled at Miles. "Did you

135

tell them anything about that incident?"

Miles stared at him, wondering what he could mean.

"In the woods. When I responded...when I grew upset."

A surge of anger hit Miles. "I would never do such a thing. No servant's gossip, sir, on any subject pertaining to you."

The dark brows smoothed. "Do calm yourself, Kenway. Miles. I apologize. I simply wonder why the servants should act as if I am such a delicate creature."

"Perhaps they treat you with kid gloves because they're worried they might be sacked. If you decide to sell the abbey, their livelihoods are in jeopardy." Miles hauled in a long breath to settle his anger. A patient man shouldn't grow so annoyed so quickly, but, for good or ill, Gerard had a way of dancing on his nerves that no one else had.

Gerard handed over the neatly stacked pile of boy's garments as he seemed to consider Miles' words. "I'm afraid I hadn't really considered that."

"Oi! Ho!"

"Coming, Ipsial." Gerard opened the door and began to laugh.

A huge puddle of water lay on the floor around the boy who'd wrapped himself in a giant Turkish towel.

"What the devil?" Miles asked, then noticed the dark cloth below the towel. The boy still wore his trousers, which were now dripping wet. The rest of his clothes floated in the water that was darkened with dirt.

"I'm clean and so's my togs," Ipsial said proudly.

"Next time do not worry about your clothing, son. We have servants to see to it." Still chuckling, Gerard grabbed another bathing towel and dropped it to the floor to soak up the puddle.

He put one hand on the boy's shoulder and led him to the

door, pausing only to take back the clothes from Miles. "Would you care to meet us down in the study so you can see Ipsial in his new clothing?"

"Yes. Thank you, sir. You, ah, might want to check behind his ears and his neck. I'm not certain they're as clean as could be."

The two of them, Ipsial and Gerard, gave him the identical bemused expression. The same blood ran in their veins.

"I'll take him to my room and use the washbowl there. The abbey is a charming mix of centuries, and though there is some plumbing in this part of the building, we still have water delivered to our rooms," he said conversationally as he led Ipsial down the hall. He sounded like a man giving a guest a tour rather than a serious adult addressing a thoroughly sodden and dripping child.

Miles turned to the mess on the floor and in the tub. Mrs. Billings would send a housemaid to tidy the room, but he supposed he could take care of the worst. A small string lay under the towel that Gerard had dropped to the floor. Attached to the grubby string was a man's pocket watch. Ipsial must have worn it on the inside of his clothing around his neck, because Miles had never noticed it. The back of the watch bore elaborate engraved initials—HG.

Miles held up the silver thing. It didn't tick, and when he gave it a small shake, he heard a rattle. He pulled on his jacket and tucked the watch away. He eyed the dreadful clothes Ipsial had been wearing and decided he'd dispose of the rags.

By the time he'd bundled up the clothes, Mrs. Billings had reappeared to take over the task.

"Thank you, Mr. Kenway. This is not at all the sort of work I'd ask of you normally. I'm embarrassed that I had to, but that Mr. Farley..." She shook her head. "You go on to the study where Mr. Gerard is waiting. I only hope that young Ipsial shan't put up such a fuss next time he requires a bath." She clasped her hands in front of her, at her waist—and he recognized her sign that she held back strong emotion.

"Mrs. Billings? Do you require more help now?"

"Yes, I shall if that boy is going to be part of this household."

"I believe Mr. Gerard's goal is to bring him here."

"If he's going to have the boy to live with him, the rumors must be true. I knew it, just looking at the lad. Mr. Gerard must be the father. Well. He should have come into the boy's life far earlier, but that's not my place to say."

Miles stayed quiet.

"It is simply that I am not good with children." She lost her self-righteousness and even seemed to deflate a bit. "Ah well, at least it seems unlikely now that the master intends to sell the place as we all feared was the case before he arrived. But I simply cannot continue to run this household on a reduced budget and with diminished staff if the family is going to be in residence."

"Indeed, you do need help. My sister shall come to us soon. Mr. Gerard declared he would hire her to take Ipsial in hand." He decided not to mention his niece and nephew.

"Your sister!" Her eyes brightened. "If she is anything like you, that should prove just the answer."

He was touched at her unexpected commendation. "As for the rest, I believe Mr. Gerard is beginning to realize what it takes to staff and maintain a house and grounds such as this. You and I shall keep working on helping him to understand, Mrs. Billings."

She gave a pleased smile at this suggestion of confederacy,

then made shooing motions with her hands. "Now do hurry, Mr. Kenway. I shan't be blamed for your dawdling."

Miles made his way down the back staircase to the study.

Long trouser-clad legs lay on the floor. A man's body prone on the carpet. Miles' heart lurched with fear. But then he moved to the sofa and saw that Ipsial sat cross-legged at the edge of the large carpet. Gerard rested on his belly, propped on elbows as he watched the boy bounce a ball on the polished parquet.

Ipsial looked paler than before. The clothes were too large, making his wrists seem spindly and his neck delicate. The features that looked attractive on Gerard were too large for the boy's small head. He'd eventually grow into that long nose and slightly pointed chin.

Miles cleared his throat to announce his presence, and Gerard scrambled to his feet. He wiped at his knees as if trying to hide the fact that he'd been sprawled on the floor. "Ipsial here is going to teach me to play chucks, what we in the south would call knucklebones."

"You don't know knucklebones, sir?" Miles hadn't thought a child alive didn't know the game played with wooden bits and a ball tossed in the air.

"No." His answer was brusque, and Miles wondered at his sudden discomfort and added that to the list of secrets he planned to uncover.

Would his employer resent any attempts to dig the truth of his past from him? And why should he not? Their intimacy could not be true friendship, not when Gerard held the full power, yet Miles would not allow himself to be cowed by this disparity. He would do his work the best he knew how, and the rest of his time, well, he would simply push as far as he was allowed, just as he would with any friend. Any friend or lover— except he had not had such a thing in his life for more than a few days.

He rubbed his hands together. "Then I shall take on Ipsial and show him how the game should be played. Hmm?"

Ipsial gave him that narrow-eyed look that used to mean he would bolt but now seemed to be a challenge. "G'wan Mr. Kenway. Your fingers are too big."

Ipsial proved correct. Miles had lost much of his ability to snatch up the bits of wood. At the end of the match, he solemnly shook hands with Ipsial, who grinned as if he had been awarded a knighthood.

The boy seemed ready to leave, off on his usual mysterious pursuits on the abbey lands, but Miles stopped him. "Did you forget something after your bath, young Ipsial?"

Ipsial scowled—a familiar expression. "My old clothes? You want me to take 'em back?"

"Not them." Miles held up the string. At the bottom, the watch twisted and spun.

"That!" Ipsial's eyes went even narrower. "That's mine. Gimme that."

"May I see it?" Gerard quickly grabbed the watch, so the question was only a matter of form.

Ipsial growled with frustration. He eyed the door as if getting ready to flee the room. He muttered something.

"Beg pardon?" Miles asked.

"I didn't steal it." The chin went up into the air. "It's mine. Me mum gave it me."

"Of course," Gerard agreed mildly as he looked it over and clicked open the back. He closed the watch and held it out to the boy, who snatched it as if grabbing it from a fire.

"It doesn't work. Probably hasn't for quite a while," Gerard said. "There's rust inside it."

140

"It's mine. It was me mum's." Clearly the fact that he'd forgotten the little keepsake rattled Ipsial—and probably the fear they'd accuse him of stealing. Ipsial's nervous response raised Mile's suspicions. He tried to think of a way of discovering the truth without driving Ipsial away, when Gerard spoke.

"Yes, I believe the watch must be yours," he said gravely. "You should take care of it, and if you ever want to fix it, let me know, and I'll cover the cost of repair, if it can be done."

Ipsial opened his cupped hands to stare down at the cheap silver watch. "Maybe," he said after a long pause. He carefully put the string over his head and around his neck, testing the strength of it.

"Will you care to join us for dinner?" Gerard asked. "We'll have lamb and small potatoes."

Ipsial swallowed and wiped the back of his hand over his mouth. "Maybe," he said.

"I believe that Mrs. Billings and the cook need to know exactly how many we can expect for a meal, so we require a firm answer." Gerard didn't scold.

"Maybe yes," Ipsial said.

That must have satisfied Gerard—he nodded. Ipsial shoved the ball and bits of wood into his coat pocket. "Want to place a wager on the next game?" the boy asked Miles.

"We shall see."

Ipsial left without another word. At least he vanished without running out of the room.

No gratitude for the clothes or the returned watch. He might be cleaner, but they had a great deal of work ahead of them if they wanted to civilize the boy. Miles wondered when Molly would arrive.

He said, "How did you know the watch belonged to Ipsial, sir? You seemed confident. I confess I'm not as certain he didn't steal it."

"I think I'd seen the watch before, years ago, when I was thirteen. It's a bit of gimcrackery presented to a boy by his mother." His voice was quiet, lost in memory.

"Someone you knew at school?"

He nodded. "And elsewhere, unfortunately. If it's the one I recall, it once belonged to my cousin Hubert Gerard."

Chapter Thirteen

Well, there was one mystery solved. Gerard tried to sort out how he felt about discovering Cousin Hubert's watch in the boy's possession. Rather relieved to know with near certainty that Ipsial wasn't his half brother, but also oddly disappointed to learn the nurturing kinship he'd begun to feel toward Ipsial was unfounded. True, the lad was still related to him, but he was Hubert's son, Hubert's direct descendent, and therefore Hubert's responsibility. The vague plans Gerard had begun to form concerning Ipsial's future were not his to make. By all rights, he should send a message to his cousin immediately and let him know about his unexpected progeny. But would Halfwit Hubie even care?

"Your cousin!" Miles exclaimed. "Are you certain?"

Gerard pushed himself up off the carpet and took a seat, motioning Miles to the other. He hadn't meant to reveal so much family business to the bailiff, but then, Miles Kenway was more than just "the bailiff" now, wasn't he? In the mere handful of hours Gerard had known him, Miles had become much more to him. Lover. Confidant. Friend.

Besides, Miles knew about the watch. It was too late to ignore the topic.

"While his paternity may never be established, I can say for certain that Ipsial couldn't possibly be mine," Gerard admitted. "I haven't been to Cambridge in years, and besides"—he cast a sloe-eyed look at Miles—"I think you are proof of the extent of my interest in women."

"You haven't ever...?"

"Never. Not even as an experiment." He tapped his fingers on the chair arm and considered asking Miles the same question, but this wasn't the time. "At any rate, I'd rather assumed my father was the culprit, sowing random seeds late in his life, but the watch seems to point rather explicitly toward Hubert."

Miles frowned at his worn boots and then looked up at Gerard. "Do you plan to send Ipsial on to him, then? Or inform him so he can come here and see the lad?"

"That's the question, isn't it? I know I ought to do one or the other, and yet I find I don't want to do either. The truth is I couldn't imagine a worse father for Ipsial if I tried. I can almost guarantee Hubert will deny paternity and reject the child completely. On the other hand, the man has only one daughter as an heir, and I could imagine him taking pride in having produced a son, albeit a bastard. Halfwit Hubie claiming Ipsial as his ward and trying to mold such an unusual child would not end well. If Ipsial didn't simply run away, he might possibly kill the man, and I'd not blame him but other people might."

Miles's lips twitched in a sardonic smile. "Sounds as if there's no love lost between you and your cousin."

"We attended school together. He was a few forms above mine. Hubert hung me with the moniker 'Eve' and led his friends in persecuting me. My cousin, who should've been my protector, or at the very least ignored me as one does a younger relative, seemed bent on making my life hell. To this day, I don't know why."

Gerard grimaced as a memory popped into his mind. "Or perhaps I do. It may have had something to do with the tricks I played on him when I was forced to stay with his family during term breaks. A lizard in Hubie's boot and water poured into his bed at night so he thought he'd wet himself—yes, I can see why he'd detest me."

"Your chickens came home to roost," Miles said.

"Nasty, pecking things." Gerard sighed. "But I suppose Hubie's teasing did no lasting harm and, if anything, made me stronger. And, let me tell you, nothing was more satisfying than the day I bested Hubie in a fight—right in front of his mates too. I came away with a black eye and a broken nose"—he indicated the slight crookedness he still wore as a battle scar—"but I felt like the king of the school."

"Do you truly believe this man hasn't matured since then? You have."

"Have I?" Gerard gave a pointed glance at the bruise on his cheek, a souvenir of their fight. "But I doubt Hubie has changed for the better. Even then I could see the framework for the sort of person Hubert would become. My dealings with him since then didn't leave me with a better impression."

"Do you think he might misuse Ipsial, should he decide to claim him?"

Gerard shrugged. "I can't imagine him spoiling the child and sparing the rod, and we both know how Ipsy responds to any threat of personal violence, even if it's perceived and not real."

Miles nodded. "I would guess the boy's been beaten often, the way he shies away when I reach toward him. We certainly wouldn't want him in a situation where he'd be abused again."

We. Gerard nearly smiled at the comfortable sound of that word. How had it happened that he and Miles had become a team of sorts in dealing with Ipsial? And why was it he could only imagine a future with Ipsial that included Miles as well?

"No, definitely not," Gerard replied. "So you see my difficulty. Is it right to contact my cousin, or should I continue

145

to care for Ipsial myself?"

"I couldn't advise you on that, sir, but I tend to believe that honesty is always best. Lies, even those of omission, tend to come back to haunt one later." Miles unfolded his long frame from the small chair and stretched to his full height. "I must tend to my duties now. There's a list of tasks as long as my arm that requires my attention today."

"Ah yes, a bailiff's work is never done." Gerard rose too. He was very reluctant to let Miles go. The day would drag long and slow if he were left to his own devices. "Might I ride out with you as you see to the estate? It's past time I learned about the land I'm responsible for. Even if I decide to sell, I should become more familiar with the property and all the upkeep it entails."

"Of course, sir. Shall we tour tomorrow morning?"

Gerard had meant immediately, as Miles well knew, and the bailiff's expression was not exactly welcoming. Where was the easy camaraderie of only minutes earlier? Gerard felt he was imposing on the man's precious time. He was as needy as a youth with an infatuation and didn't like the way his insides felt all weak and churning. But he didn't wish to withdraw his request.

"Yes, that will be good," he conceded.

Kenway gave a short bow and left without looking back. Of course Gerard knew this, because he watched every step the man took as he walked away.

He would not loll about the study, pining and frustrated. For a few minutes, he considered strolling about the grounds again, testing himself against the poison of the memories, but the soft patter of rain changed his mind. Instead, he went to the kitchen to inform the newly hired cook's assistant they might expect Ipsial for dinner.

A bit later, Farley found him in the library and began to

complain about Mrs. Billings.

Gerard interrupted his listing of her deficiencies. "She has enough to do, and her work increases when I'm in residence. I think perhaps we'll need to hire a couple more servants."

"More servants? Aren't we going back to London soon?"

The wind picked up and rain rattled against the glass. Farley gave a significant glance at the window as if the weather argued for their return to civilization.

Gerard felt as if someone—Farley? The abbey?—had placed a wager against him. *You do not have the courage to remain.*

He couldn't abide losing. "We shall see."

He wasn't surprised when Ipsial didn't come to dinner. The boy needed warmer clothes, perhaps an oilcloth coat, before he should have to face this sort of weather. For a few minutes, Gerard contemplated going out into the windy darkness and finding him, and bringing him to the shelter of the house. But Ipsial must come in his own time.

He stared out the window and tried not to imagine the boy dripping wet, shivering, huddled in a broken-down abandoned building. The abbey still proved a harsh environment for children.

The next morning dawned overcast. Gerard woke and dressed early and still found Kenway waiting for him.

"Good morning." The bailiff's deep voice sounded cheery for such an early hour. Was he the sort of man who rose before the sun, whistling? Gerard shuddered at the thought.

They walked to the stable, discussing which man from the village might prove a reliable groom. Joey had more than enough work. In addition to the new kitchen maid, more help for Mrs. Billings was needed. Gerard could afford to pay all these positions as well as for the repairs. He no longer wished to starve the abbey as if it were a malevolent creature or allow it to crumble into the ground. Was it possible that this new feeling stirring inside him was pride of ownership?

He and Kenway were soon on horseback, talking about crops, the amount of game taken from the woods and the need for repairs on an old stone wall. Kenway introduced an entirely new language for Gerard: the vocabulary of the landowner.

They drew near the woods, and at last the dreary familiar apprehension hit. Gerard knew how quickly that apprehension could mount to a heart-pounding shortness of breath, so he concentrated on observing his surroundings and listening as Kenway talked about a blockage in the stream which should be cleared before the spring flood season.

"Yes, of course you shall have funds for the work." Gerard sounded far too warm and grateful for such a mundane topic, but, with the crutch of Kenway's deep voice to steady him, he'd managed to fight off the confounded fear.

"Very good, sir." Kenway sounded as if he cheered Gerard on, and perhaps he did. For a moment, his encouragement seemed an insult. Gerard was his master, not some small lad facing the dark. But Kenway's enthusiasm was too genuine— Gerard would be churlish to grow offended.

The day became pleasant, bright blue skies with an occasional cloud scudding across, and the waving grass of the moor was a lovely golden-brown this autumn day.

"Beautiful countryside. I'd forgotten how beautiful it can be when it's not gray and rainy," Gerard said as he gazed across the land—his land now—and felt another surge of possessive pride.

"It'll do," Miles said, a typically laconic Yorkshire response.

Gerard guided his roan around a caved-in spot and glanced over at the big man atop an enormous bay horse. "Do you like the country here, or do you prefer Yorkshire, or Canada?"

"Each has its merits I suspect." Miles pointed to the south. "We'll be stopping in to see Edward Cage. The old duffer is in arrears on rent, but there's not much can be done about it. His mind is wandering, and he has no one to tend him in his final days. Neighbors drop in from time to time, but I like to check on him nearly every day to make certain he's eaten and hasn't fallen down his well or something."

"That's kind of you, and I'm certainly happy to forego the man's rent under the circumstances."

Gerard was once again reminded of the difference between himself and his employee. This land belonged to him. Miles only managed it. What would happen if he were to sell the land to someone who might not be so charitable to an old coot with dim wits, and what if a different bailiff took over who didn't look the other way? For the first time, he truly understood how much his tenants relied on him.

Gerard took another look around him at the land, which seemed to be holding him in invisible filaments like a spider's web. Not so easy to break free after all. He glanced at Miles's broad back posting up and down in perfect harmony with the bay. But then perhaps that wasn't a bad thing.

Miles was acutely aware of Gerard's gaze on him and his presence beside him as he went about his routine tasks of overseeing the abbey lands. It felt strange to be observed and perhaps judged by his employer as he performed his duties. And, of course, he couldn't stop thinking about Gerard in other capacities besides employer. Their joining yesterday had been... He simply had no words for it, nothing that didn't sound poetical and overwrought, at any rate. Sublime. Deeply moving. Raw and primeval. Transcendent yet as earthy as a pig rolling in mud. Good thing he wasn't a poet, because he'd do a damn poor job of describing what that union had been like for him.

The bay stumbled, and because Miles wasn't paying attention, he nearly lost his seat. He straightened his back and his composure and led on to the next task on his list.

When they'd stopped to see Edward Cage, the old man had been dining on cold soup provided by a neighbor and was in a fairly lucid state for once. Gerard had been kind and friendly, squatting so he could meet Edward's gaze and speaking slowly to be sure he understood. Despite his occasionally pugnacious manner, the man certainly had a nurturing side and was a natural with both the elderly and children. It had warmed Miles's heart to watch him.

Now they were nearing the spot where a fallen tree was slowing the flow of the stream that meandered across the moor in many directions. The brook supplied indispensable water for flocks of sheep and for irrigation. Due to the natural dam, water was starting to back up and change course. The downed tree needed to be removed soon.

He dismounted from Pegasus and squelched through the marshy land around the watercourse, his waders tossing up droplets of muddy water. Gerard and his pristine riding boots kept their distance as he held the horses' reins.

"Do you hear that?" Gerard called over the burble of water. "A bleating on the other side of the fallen tree."

Miles did hear and followed the sound to where a young lamb had gotten tangled in branches. It was the lamb the farmer called Miracle, the only lamb he or Miles had ever heard of to be born in the autumn. The poor thing was so covered in mud that its pale wool appeared black. As Miles drew near, the animal flailed helplessly and let out another pitiful bleat.

"There. There. Easy now," Miles crooned as he stooped to free hooves and legs from the branches and mud.

"Can I help?" Gerard had come closer, leading the horses to the edge of the swampy ground.

"No. Stay back lest the horses get stuck in the mud," Miles cautioned. "I'm almost done here." With that he finished disentangling the lamb and lifted its squirming body in his arms. A sharp little hoof dug into his chest as the creature kicked him. "Shush now. Be still," he commanded softly. "How did you wander so far from your mother? Why isn't she sounding the alarm?"

"Aw, the poor thing. It must be half drowned," Gerard said.

Miles took off his scarf and wrapped it around the lamb to stop its kicking, then tucked the sodden body into the front of his coat. "He'll live. Just need to get him back to his flock." Miles mounted Pegasus with some difficulty as the lamb continued to fight its rescuer.

"How do you know where it belongs?"

"This one? Ah, this baby, born now—that's as rare as hen's teeth. They always come all at once, sir. You should see the lambs in early spring, sir. Lambing season is magical."

Gerard chuckled. "You sound besotted."

"I am, at that."

The lamb wiggled and gave a plaintive cry.

"Shouldn't we take it home, warm it by a fire and give it something to eat first?" Gerard asked as he gracefully vaulted onto the back of the roan.

"Nay. I don't think it's been stuck long. Best we can do is let it find its mother's teat." Grinning to himself at the master's softhearted response, Miles led the way across the open land to the nearest flock of grazing sheep.

Dismounting again, he unwrapped and released the wet animal. Still bawling about its recent brush with death, it bounded toward the others. Its mother answered the call, and they were soon reunited.

He looked at Gerard, standing beside him. "And so life goes on, eh?"

Gerard glanced at him. "You're a disaster."

Miles cast a rueful eye at his ruined shirt and soaking-wet coat. "I guess I need to return home and change." He met Gerard's gaze. "Maybe we can have a cup of hot rum to warm us up."

And after that? Oh God, he could imagine Gerard lying naked on his bed, arms folded behind his head, eyes mischievous as they enticed Miles to join him. The thought of having this man in his cottage, in his own bed, was so exciting Miles could scarcely breathe. His heart was as light as the lark swooping overhead. He felt he might break into song like the bird, then lift off the earth and fly away.

"I would *love* to have a drink or two with you," Gerard replied as a slow smile lit his face. "Can the estate do without you for a bit?"

"I'm afraid it must," Miles teased in return. It was embarrassing how he lost all sense of propriety in Gerard's vicinity and wanted nothing more than to strip to his skin and tumble the other man roughly onto his bed. He had little doubt that was what was going to happen next.

Chapter Fourteen

At the cottage, Gerard stood and watched Miles pour buckets of water into a cast iron pot that swung over the fire.

"You should have allowed me to help fetch the water. You're shivering so, I can hear your teeth rattle."

Miles paused as he peeled off his shirt, leaving him in only a vest and thick trousers. "No."

Gerard gave a cluck of disgust. "Your objection had best not be because of our differences in station."

"Not at all. Moving keeps me from turning into a pillar of ice. Who'd have thought such a pleasant day could turn so chilly?"

"That's bloody England for you. I miss Italy." What would Miles think of Florence? Gerard imagined showing him his favorite cities, and they could soak up the sun in the south perhaps in Siderno. He would most definitely not introduce him to Azzari or his crowd.

Fantasy, he reminded himself. Back to reality, which seemed more than entertaining enough. Gerard moved toward Miles, hands outstretched. "While the water heats, allow me to warm you, Kenway."

The man paused, looked at Gerard's hands, then up at his face, a smile slowly spreading from his eyes to his mouth. "You might call me Miles. Sir."

"And I've already invited you to call me Gerard, as my friends do." He nearly said *I've already instructed you*, but that was too close to an order.

"We are friends?" Miles sounded slightly troubled.

"Yes, we are." His breath felt rough in his throat. He took Miles's broad hand in his own and ran his fingers over the hard palm and blunt fingertips, lightly scuffing, pretending to warm him, but in truth feeling the callused firm flesh. Until Miles shivered again.

Gerard stepped closer and pulled him into his arms. "I recall reading that when one encounters a person in danger of freezing to death, one should remove all clothing from both bodies and wrap tight together in blankets."

"I'm all over mud."

"Now I am too."

Miles twisted in his embrace.

He released his arms reluctantly, then gasped as Miles cupped his face in those ice-cold hands and pressed his mouth to Gerard's. Miles's nose and lips were chilly but warmed almost at once. So did Gerard's insides as he heard that soft growl, already familiar, signaling Miles's arousal.

"You taste so delicious." Miles's voice was low and gritty with desire.

They kissed, pulled away to examine each other, then returned to deeper, more complex kisses. Gerard had never explored so hungrily, even with his eager Italian. The small nips and brushes of lips sank into ravenous open-mouthed feasting. Miles's hard body rubbed Gerard's harder erection. He craved release but sensed a different sort of tension in Miles.

"Mm." He pressed a kiss to Miles's neck and rested his cheek on his shoulder. More time had passed than Gerard had thought possible—steam vigorously rose from the cauldron over the fire.

Miles pulled away. He cleared his throat and passed a hand through his hair, then glanced at his hand and wrinkled his nose. "I'll wash off the worst of the dirt."

"Shall I help?"

"No. I'll go fast."

"If you insist." Gerard backed up until his legs hit the edge of the chair by one side of the fire. He settled in to watch Miles clean up.

The door creaked.

Miles wrapped the towel around his neck. "Who's there?"

A small, peaked face peered in at them. "You smell like a bog." Ipsial's young voice sounded full of scorn.

Gerard swallowed his urge to yelp or shout. Christ, what if Miles had taken him up on his offer of help? That would be twice the boy would've caught them in a compromising situation. "You must learn to knock on doors, boy."

The boy curled his lip. "Something you don't want me to see?"

Gerard wouldn't show how the sly question worried him. He clenched his teeth tightly and managed to speak without cursing. "It's good manners to knock, Ipsial. You must be polite so you will get along in the world. Life is easier for those who follow rules of behavior."

"Oh." Ipsial reached down and rubbed a finger on his well-polished shoe. He looked up into Gerard's face for an instant, then looked away. "Sorry."

An apology from Ipsial? A choir of angels did not sing hallelujah, but it was a close thing. Miles's eyes met Gerard's and widened. He seemed more amused than worried.

Gerard managed to quiet his own response. "As long as you can remember to knock at closed doors and wait for a response, then all is forgiven."

Ipsial wrinkled his nose. "Suppose."

Miles reached for a shirt on the other chair by the fire and pulled it on. "Would you care for some dinner, Ipsial?" He looked at Gerard uncertainly. "Finer folk might call it luncheon, I suppose?"

"Hm. Yes." Gerard fought a surge of angry disappointment. He'd craved Miles and looked forward to tasting his clean skin. Alas, this was the life of a man with a family.

A family?

"Are you all right, sir?" Miles asked. "You look slightly upset."

He forced himself to smile. "Certainly. May I stay and share your dinner, Mr. Kenway? Ipsial?"

"Why?"

"Why what, Ipsial?"

"You eat lamb up at the house. Mr. Kenway never got nothing but tough old mutton."

"Lesson two of good manners. Never criticize your host's cooking."

"He cooks fine. But mutton isn't lamb."

"If he should serve you an old boot or a chunk of wood, you should say, 'Thank you, sir'."

Ipsial snorted.

"It's true," Gerard insisted.

"Wood?" The boy's scorn was obvious.

"It's true," Miles repeated. "If you're served kindling, you say, 'My, this oak looks appetizing'. You don't have to eat it, mind. Just scrap at it a bit with your knife. Chew on a bit o' the bark. Spit it out in your napkin when no one's watching."

An honest to goodness giggle erupted from Ipsial, the first Gerard had heard.

Gerard exchanged another glance with Miles, who wore such wide grin it forced a smile in answer. He looked forward to this meal almost as much as he had anticipated the passion he'd planned to share with Miles.

They sat at the plain wooden table. Miles produced three mismatched bowls and filled them with stew he warmed over the fire.

"You'll burn your fingers," he warned Ipsial, who reached into his bowl.

"Don't mind."

"I do," Miles said blandly.

They managed to coax the boy to use a spoon, but he didn't like the fork. Miles wisely didn't offer the knife. Ipsial had appalling manners, of course, but Gerard decided those could come later.

"Mrrfwf. Faah," Ipsial said around a mouth full of food. He looked at Gerard expectantly.

"I beg your pardon? If you swallow, perhaps sip some water and ask again, I might understand you."

Ipsial picked up the mug and gulped down the water. "Are you my da?"

Gerard had been expecting the question, just not so suddenly or bluntly asked. Should he tell the truth? He suspected that the boy had drawn closer and allowed him liberties—such as the bath—because Ipsial believed Gerard was his father.

"Would you like such a thing?" he asked.

Ipsial shrugged. He shoved more food into his mouth. "Oo?"

Before Gerard could speak, Ipsial swallowed, drank and said, "You didn't know about me?"

"No. I didn't. I came here as soon as I learned of your existence." That was close enough to the truth.

"You glad?"

"Yes, I am very glad I came here." And that was entirely true. He cleared his throat. "I should like to make sure you are safe, Ipsial. I want to help you. But I want you to agree to certain conditions."

Ipsial stirred the stew and picked out a chunk of meat. "What d'you mean?"

"I shall make a list of what I expect from you."

"A list." Ipsial scowled and popped the meat in his mouth.

"And you should make a list of your own. Of what you want."

"'Ors," Ipsial said around the meat.

"We can discuss a horse, but I wish to discover what you're interested in, where you'd like to live, that sort of thing."

"Wi' my da, of course," Ipsial said. "With you."

Dread and delight filled Gerard, and he wondered which emotion would win. "Do you have paper, Mr. Kenway?"

Miles nodded. He fetched a pen, ink and several sheets of cheap paper from a small table by his bed.

Gerard pushed his bowl and cup aside, opened the ink bottle and dipped his pen. "I shall write my list first."

Ipsial watched, fascinated, mouth slightly ajar.

Gerard scratched out the words.

"That my name?" Ipsial pointed at the word *Agree*.

"No. And we should add that condition to the list. I shall

read to you until you learn to read on your own. Here's what I wrote. I, Everett Micah Josiah Gerard—"

He ignored Miles's muttered, "Micah Josiah?"

"—Gerard agree to provide you, Ipsial Gerard, with food, shelter and an education. In return, you shall obey these rules. No stealing. No lying. No running away. You will allow me and Mr. Kenway to instruct you in the proper ways to behave."

"I'm a good boy," Ipsial said promptly. Gerard nodded, glad because someone had obviously given Ipsial the gift of those words.

"Indeed. Clever as well. Not many lads could have come all that way on their own." He dipped the nib, pulled a handkerchief from his pocket and absently blotted the pen. Ipsial and Kenway both protested that he should treat such a fine piece of clothing so badly.

"Likely I need to instruct you," Ipsial said with disapproval.

"You must not correct your elders," Gerard said gently.

"Even when they are fools?"

"Perhaps if they are in danger, but otherwise, it is not done."

"Huh." Ipsial turned and spat.

"And you should not spit indoors."

Ipsial wrinkled his freckled nose. It gave him the appearance of disgust, but Gerard had learned it was his habit when confused. "I know. Forgot it."

Gerard hid a smile. "We won't write that one down, then."

"If I forget and do bad things, what'll happen?"

Before Gerard could think of a good answer, Ipsial said, "I ain't going to the poorhouse. I hate that place. I'd run off."

"No, no," Gerard said. He touched Ipsial's arm and

pretended not to notice how the boy flinched.

Ipsial stared at the page. "Them's so many words. What'll you do if I fail?"

"You shan't fail," Miles said and gave Gerard a stern look. "You shall make mistakes and break rules, but you will learn and grow and make fewer mistakes each day."

"If I don't," Ipsial practically wailed. His croaking voice cracked. "If I don't learn."

"Then we will have been bad teachers. You are clever; you want to improve. If you don't learn, it will be our fault, not yours." Miles's deep voice easily drowned out his sobs. "Come, come, lad. You do your best, and we shall be satisfied. More than satisfied, glad to have you."

Ipsial rose from the chair.

"Come here," Miles coaxed.

Ipsial let him pull him onto his lap. The boy buried his face in his chest and shook.

"I have failed already," Gerard said in quiet despair. "I wished to make the situation easy to understand, but I have only overwhelmed him."

Miles made a scornful sound. "You are both too frightened. He knows you mean well, sir. And look, here now is my lad Ipsial letting me hold him. He hasn't before, have you?"

Ipsial didn't seem to be listening, but Miles went on. "He knows he's safe enough now, and he can just be a boy."

That got Ipsial to pull back. "I'm big. I'm not crying." He blinked his reddened eyes and glared at them both. He hiccupped.

"Of course not," Miles said. "No one would say so."

Miles shot a fast smile at Gerard, who felt such gratitude he wanted to break down and sob in his arms too.

"A'right, then," Ipsial said drowsily. "I'll stay wi' Da."

Da. Gerard stopped breathing for a moment. What had he gotten himself into?

"It'll be a grand new life," Miles said as if he'd read his thoughts.

"Yes, of course," Gerard said. "And your sister will be on her way soon, Mr. Kenway?"

Miles laughed.

They fell silent, and Gerard stared into the fire, wondering what he could have done differently. He'd have more chances, because Ipsial wouldn't run away. That was a relief.

Sprawled in Miles's arms, Ipsial made a small sound. A snore.

"Good Lord, he fell asleep quickly," Gerard whispered.

"A full stomach, a comfortable place." Miles didn't bother to lower his voice. He casually hitched the limp body so the boy lay more comfortably.

The pale face looked so much younger in repose.

Guilt washed through Gerard. "I worried about him in the rain last night, but I hadn't realized how close he was to giving in to the campaign to civilize him. I wish I had gone out to look for him." Gerard sighed. "It's settled, then. I shan't tell that dastard Hubert about the boy."

"Are you sure he doesn't already know about his existence?"

"Who's Hubert?" The sleepy voice came from Miles's arms.

"No one you need worry about," Gerard said. "Go to sleep."

"A'right."

Lesson one. Never assume Ipsial wasn't listening to every word spoken in front of him. Gerard picked up the pen and scratched the words, *I want you,* on one of the blank pieces of paper. He showed it to Miles, who nodded slowly.

Miles said, "You shall stay at the abbey for a time?"

"Yes, I think I must. No plans to sell for the present."

"Good." Miles's slow smile was full of wicked intentions, Gerard hoped.

He wrote: *I would strip you naked and kiss every inch of your skin, every hair on your body.*

Miles blushed and gave a quick shake of the head. He looked as if he wanted to protest.

"Well?" Gerard demanded.

"Yes. *Another* time, sir."

It was Gerard's turn to grin as he slowly crumpled the paper and tossed it into the fire.

Gerard's usual restless manner had vanished, as if he'd never paced a room, sought a fight or challenged himself by climbing a mountain. It was only the middle of the day, but he felt as relaxed as he did when it was late at night and he'd drunk most of a decanter of brandy. His bones were heavier than usual. This was Miles's influence. Any man, or boy, who'd been on guard and alert for danger for days, or even years, could stand down. Miles would keep them safe, he thought, drowsy and comfortable.

"You too, sir? Would you care to stretch out on my bed?"

Only with you, he thought but did not dare say with Ipsial in the vicinity. He yawned. "Thank you, no. I am content." And that was the apt word, was it not? He had known Miles for less than a week, but the mere presence of the man did more for his spirit than the sprightliest conversations with other men. Since his father's death, he'd been seeking something as he gallivanted about Europe. He hadn't known exactly what.

Sexual encounters and liquor and playing fast and loose with his fortune hadn't fulfilled this need. Miles Kenway might be the answer.

Chapter Fifteen

Children should be seen and not heard.

Gerard thought a better saying might be, *Children should disappear when they're inconvenient.* Or at least have a lever to turn them off. Now that he and Miles had got Ipsial talking, they couldn't seem to find that switch. Over the past couple of weeks since the breakthrough moment with Ipsial in Miles's cottage, a constant stream of thoughts bubbled out of the boy's head and then his mouth in a never-ending fountain. It made Gerard wonder how many years he'd been holding back those ideas and insights—no one to share them with. Gerard understood, having had a similar isolated boyhood, at least until he'd made a set of chums at boarding school.

In truth, he was glad Ipsial had changed almost overnight from a sullen, taciturn ruffian into a chatty, inquisitive boy, but it certainly was hard to find time to be alone with Miles for any meaningful length of time. Ipsial was always *there*. Right there. Stuck to one or both of them like a burr. It gladdened Gerard's heart that the boy seemed to have placed his trust in them. If only he weren't quite so needy. But he supposed being a father—a good father, not one like his own had been—meant being approachable, especially for a child like Ipsial who'd had such a hard life.

Gerard straightened the knot on his tie, ran a brush through his hair one last time and turned from the looking glass to leave his bedroom. He opened the door and found Ipsial waiting for him on the other side, owlish eyes staring unblinking at him.

"You said we'd have a riding lesson today."

"That's right. I did. But I didn't say when, now did I? It's still very early. Have you been down to breakfast?"

"Long time ago." Ipsial dragged a toe of the new riding boots Gerard had purchased for him over the carpet.

"Well, I haven't. Why don't you go out to the stable and ask Joey to saddle Barley and start on your lesson? I'll be there as soon as I'm finished, and we can go on a proper ride."

Ipsial frowned and dug his toe deeper into the thick carpet. "I might wait for you." The boy was clearly torn between his eagerness to get to the horse and his desire to stay close to Gerard.

"It's all right to go on ahead. I promise I'll join you," Gerard said gently but firmly.

Ipsy looked up and nodded gravely. "Right, then." With that, he trotted away, boots thumping on the wood.

Gerard exhaled in relief. They'd have to work on Ipsial's fear of separation. Such an unexpected contrast to the child he'd first met, who couldn't be contained any more than a wild thing could be.

All I can do is let him know he can trust me not to desert him, he thought as he descended the stairs.

Indeed, he was late to breakfast as the toast had gone cold and the tea was tepid. By the time the maid came in with a fresh pot, Gerard waved her away. "Don't bother. I'm in a hurry to get outdoors."

The bug-eyed girl always appeared worried, afraid she'd displease and lose her new position. Gerard smiled to put her fears to rest and then strode out to greet the new day.

He gazed across the grounds and took a deep breath of the

crisp air, chilled enough to make his nose tingle. Ah, country life really was wonderful after all. And today—sometime today, no matter what it took—he would get those moments alone with Miles that he'd been denied over the past few weeks. Yes, they had seized an occasional kiss in an alcove or behind a tree, but there'd been no time for more than a quick grope, and Gerard was getting desperate.

Was Miles missing him too? Longing for him in his narrow bed in the shabby cottage while Gerard tossed and turned in his four-poster in the abbey? Several times, Gerard had come very close to slipping out to meet his lover in the wee hours of the morning. But with Ipsial so newly ensconced indoors, he'd hesitated to leave the house. What if the boy awoke and needed him?

Tonight he'd worry about that no longer. Tonight he and Miles would be together once more. They'd take their time and explore each other at leisure. The thought of it thrummed through his veins and put a huge smile on his face as he walked toward the stable yard.

Joey held a tether line and turned in a slow circle as Barley plodded diligently around him, a very proud Ipsial perched on the old horse's back.

"Good form," Gerard called to the boy and leaned against the fence, resting his arms on the top rail. "I see you've got your back straight and heels down as you've been taught."

Ipsial glanced over at him and grinned.

Gerard felt a surge of pride as if he were the boy's actual father. *Why, he's quite a handsome little lad.* Without his permanent scowl, the overly large features Ipsial hadn't quite grown into didn't appear so homely.

"Tired of going in circles. Can we go on a real ride now?" Ipsial asked.

"May we," Gerard corrected automatically. "I suppose we might."

He told Joey to keep tending to Ipsial and went to saddle his own mount. The unpolished state of the tack underlined the need for a stable hand to help the groom. Gerard pictured the stables brought up to snuff, modernized along with the rest of the ancient abbey. His vision of the future made him aware he'd already made a decision to stay for more than just a short while. He wasn't going anywhere, not anymore.

Gerard had only just mounted the roan, unoriginally named Star for the white blaze on its forehead, and Joey was giving Ipsial a few instructions as the boy rode out of the corral, when the unmistakable sound of rattling carriage wheels came from the drive. Gerard looked up as a shabby carriage drew into view. No reason for the sense of dread that prickled the hairs on his neck as the vehicle came to a halt. Perhaps it was a neighbor from one of the other estates who'd come to call, but he thought he recognized the coach for hire at the train station.

"Hold up, Ipsial," he ordered as the boy rode up beside him. "We have a visitor."

"Who's that?" Ipsial's tone was flat and his expression tense, a return to the wary child Gerard had first met.

"I don't know yet. But it's a guest, and we have to greet..." He broke off as the driver opened the door and a man stepped out. "Oh, hell."

"Who is it?" the child repeated.

"My cousin, Hubert."

"The one you don't like." Ipsial revealed again that it was never safe to talk in front of a child, even if one assumed he was asleep.

"Hush now," Gerard warned as he slid from the saddle to the ground. "We won't be able to ride right now. I want you to go back to the stable with Joey and stay there. Help him groom the horses until I send for you. Do you understand?"

"Yes."

Shockingly, for once Ipsial recognized the authority in Gerard's tone and did as he was bid, turning Barley and heading back to the barn while Joey took the roan from Gerard and led him away.

Gerard exhaled a deeply held breath and strode across the yard and lawn toward the carriage. Hubert stood staring at the abbey while the driver unloaded a trunk and valise.

When he caught sight of Gerard, Hubert raised a hand in greeting. "Cousin. So good to see you. It's been far too many years with nothing but an occasional letter between us."

No letters and a good five hundred miles are fine by me. Gerard forced a friendly smile as he approached. "With so few members left in our family, we really ought to keep in better touch." He eyed the growing pile of luggage, which now included another valise. "So, have you come to stay?"

"I've been thinking about the importance of family lately and felt moved to see our family estate once more." Hubert wore a hard smile that looked disturbingly familiar. Gerard and his cousin might have been brothers, although Hubert didn't have the bump in the bridge of the nose. His nose had never been broken. Gerard's had, twice.

Gerard folded his arms. If he could face down the ghosts of the abbey, then Hubie should be easy. "Lucky your visit coincided with mine. I haven't been here in years myself."

"Oh, it was no coincidence. I ran into a mutual acquaintance of ours at my club, Rodney Dowling, who mentioned you would be here."

"I see. Good old Rodney." Gerard continued to maintain a polite smile as he waited to find out what had really brought

Hubie to the abbey. The man had to want something.

Hubert gave another assessing gaze at the rambling building. "So, what brings you to our ancestral home after all these years, Everett? Are you considering a sale?"

Ah, there it was. Hubert's use of "*our* family home" and "ancestral" seemed to indicate that he wanted a piece of the pie after it was cut. Well, that was something Gerard would be happy to deny him.

"I must say, I had thought of selling, but the house would need extensive work first. Then, after I began picturing what could be done with the place, I decided I couldn't bear to part with it after all. As you say, the Gerard family roots are here."

"Quite." Hubie's affable countenance soured a little. Then, with whiplash speed, he did an about-face on the "dear old family home" tack. "I just wanted to let you know I would have no objection to selling it and sharing the money. Despite the generations of our people who've lived and died here, it *is* only a house and land, after all, and has no real meaning for me personally. I have my own home and my own family in London."

"Yes, and it is past time I met your dear wife, Emily, and your little Jane." Gerard's cheeks were beginning to hurt from smiling. "I'm rather surprised you didn't bring them to see the place you're bidding good-bye to. But happily, they can visit another time, as I've decided not to sell."

Hubie's jaw tightened. "Is that wise? Is there any reason for a permanent bachelor such as yourself to hold on to such a large place?"

The way he sneered as he spoke the words "permanent bachelor" froze Gerard's belly. And that smile. Hubie knew.

Had that damned dissipated conte spilled his secrets? Gerard's brain scrambled around, trying to understand what he must do to keep his cousin at bay. He would say nothing, show nothing. Admit. Nothing.

In the silence that fell between them, two voices drifted crystal clear from the stable yard—Ipsial's chatter, answered by Miles's slow, deep voice.

Ipsial sounded breathless with excitement, but his voice carried. "It's the dastard, or maybe he said bastard? That's what I am."

"Not good words, Ipsial," Miles said. The boy rarely paid attention, but Miles insisted on attempting to improve his language.

"But Mr. Gerard doesn't like him. Come on, Mr. Kenway. Send him away. You're big enough to beat him to a smear."

"Hush," Miles said.

The two of them walked across the grass toward Gerard. Hubie turned and watched. His brows rose and his mouth drooped open. "Who is that little gnome of a child?"

Gerard felt enormous gratitude he hadn't told Hubie of his son's existence. He only hoped Ipsial hadn't heard him. He doubted the boy would be insulted, but he'd certainly want to lash out in return. Gerard called, "Ipsial, come say hello to Mr. Gerard."

"*You're* Mr. Gerard."

"I am Mr. Everett Gerard. This is Mr. Hubert Gerard."

"He looks a little like you, except you're better looking."

"Ipsial, say how do you do." Miles had adopted the quiet rumble that Ipsial had learned not to ignore.

"Howdoyoudosir." He turned it into one word.

Hubie wrinkled his nose—on him, it seemed to indicate disgust—and examined Ipsial. Any second now he'd see the resemblance and know. "What sort of a name is Ipsial?"

"Mine."

"Is it Biblical?"

"Dunno." The boy shrugged thin shoulders. "Me mother give it me. Said it was a proper gentleman's name."

Hubert's eyes narrowed as he stared at the boy. The man might be many annoying things but stupid wasn't one of them, despite the moniker of Halfwit Hubie that Gerard had labeled him with as a schoolboy. "How do you come to be here? How old are you, boy?"

Ipsial shrugged again, and his own eyes narrowed in an expression eerily similar to Hubert's. Gerard's pulse quickened, and he swallowed.

"Older than my Janie. About eight or nine, I would suspect. Where are you from, lad?" Hubert demanded.

Ipsial's lips clamped in a straight line, and his body tensed. If Miles's hand weren't resting on his shoulder, Gerard felt sure the child would have bolted, a wild thing once more.

"Who is your mother?" Hubert pressed as he took a step toward Ipsial.

Gerard exchanged a look with Miles. The cat was nearly out of the bag, and Gerard was more certain than ever that it was not a kitty he wanted to let Hubie play with. He opened his mouth to say something, anything, to derail this line of questioning.

Unfortunately, Miles didn't catch the meaning of his silent warning. He gave Ipsial's shoulder a light squeeze. "It's all right. You may answer him. Tell the truth."

Ipsial glanced up at Miles before locking gazes with his father again. "Jennie McCray. Cambridge."

A quick succession of expressions flitted across Hubert's face. Gerard thought he recognized remembrance, dismay, possibly disgust, and then maybe a soupcon of pride at having fathered a son. Or perhaps he was imagining all those emotions and Hubie was merely having indigestion.

"Jennie McCray. I know that name."

He turned his gaze on Gerard, who immediately shifted his attention to his sleeve; he smoothed a wrinkle and schooled his features to interested boredom. He would not give away anything to his cousin.

Hubie continued, "So what brought you to the abbey, young sir?"

Hubert sounded too jovial to be honest, and Ipsial's glare told the world he wasn't falling for the cheery tone. "The train."

Gerard decided it was past time for him to intercede. "You must be exhausted from your journey, Hubert. Why don't you come inside and refresh yourself?" He took his cousin's arm, perhaps a bit more forcefully than was necessary, and guided him toward the door. He shot a look over his shoulder at Miles—more of a frown, really—to let him know he should remove Ipsial from the equation. It would be all he could do to distract Hubert from the boy's existence, satisfy his cousin's desire for monetary gain, and get him the hell on his way again as soon as possible.

If he could manage it, Halfwit Hubie would never know for certain that the foundling on their doorstep was his son and would never lay claim to Ipsial.

Chapter Sixteen

The glare Gerard shot him as he marched his cousin indoors was so exactly like the scowl on Ipsial's face that the pair could've been mirror images of each other. Miles tugged gently on Ipsial's arm. "Come along, lad. There's work to be done, and I need your help doing it."

Over the past weeks, he'd learned that Ipsy was quite glad to help with physical chores if Miles presented the request in words that made the boy feel relied on. From the bits of his past he'd revealed in passing, it sounded as if Ipsial had fought for scraps to get by and often needed to care for his mother rather than the other way around. Poor little chap had drifted on his own for far too long. He needed a solid anchor and a firm hand to guide his rudder.

Ipsial fell into step beside him. "Why is Mr. Gerard being nice to that dastard when he doesn't even like him? Why didn't you throw him out?"

"Sometimes one has to put on a pleasant expression when dealing with people one doesn't care for. That's part of being an adult."

"But Mr. Gerard—my da—doesn't like him. What if that man, that cousin, steals something or does something bad? I don't like him either." Ipsial's voice was fierce. Protective, Miles realized.

"Don't worry. Our Mr. Gerard is a sharp one. He won't let his cousin get the upper hand, I'm sure, and I don't think you need to worry about a physical attack. That's not the way gentlemen settle arguments."

Ipsial gave him a sharp look. "You and Mr. Gerard brawled that first night."

"Well, I'm not a gentleman." It was time to change the subject lest Ipsial began to ask questions about the other things he might have seen them do that night. "Now to work. We have stones to load up and carry to the broken spot in the wall. Let us concentrate on that, and Mr. Gerard will decide how he wishes to deal with his relative."

Would Gerard tell Hubert the truth about Ipsial's watch? Would a man like Hubert want to claim such an uncouth child? Miles glanced at the boy marching stolidly beside him and felt a flash of fear. He didn't want Ipsial to be snatched away by this vulture of a man. Ipsial belonged to Miles and Gerard. They'd put a lot of work and care into him and, in the process, become attached to the little wretch. He was theirs. Why in heaven had Miles encouraged Ipsy to say anything about his past? Why had he felt the need to at least let Hubert know this might be his son? Foolish honesty! Sometimes prevarication or half-truths really were the best. No wonder Gerard had given him that disdainful glance as they'd parted.

"Don't look so worried." Miles tried to erase the gloom from Ipsial's face. "There's nothing for you to fear. I'm sure everything will turn out all right."

But he was trying to convince himself as much as the boy.

Gerard led his cousin into the sitting room rather than the study. He had pleasant memories of the study he didn't want marred by his cousin. They waited silently while the maid scurried in to light the fire.

The room was cluttered, every surface covered with lace cloths under china figurines and dusty stuffed birds in bell jars.

Two dainty armchairs stood by the fire. Clearly this had been Gerard's mother's territory, but he had no early memories of her in the room—in truth he had very few memories of her at all. Except, of course, that last one.

He wished he could banish that blind-staring bloody face from his memory.

Mrs. Billings silently entered with a tray that held decanters and two goblets. "Anything else, sir?"

"No thank you."

She cast a quick glance at Hubert and left.

Hubie scowled after her. "Was that the housekeeper serving us? Where's the butler? And not so much as a footman? Don't think I haven't noticed how you've neglected this place. At the very least, you need manservants. Or is that one we met escorting the boy enough for you?"

Gerard poured Hubie a glass of brandy. Maybe if the idiot got inebriated, he'd be less irritating and perhaps even fall asleep. That would be good.

Hubie took a big swallow of brandy and sighed with pleasure. He sat in an armchair by the fire. "So tell me, Eve, how did you end up saddled with my little bastard?"

Gerard unclenched his teeth. He sipped his drink before answering, "Do you remember what happened the last time you called me by that name?"

Gerard was delighted to see his cousin wince at the memory of their last scuffle.

Hubie sighed dramatically. "Beg pardon, of course. Such trouble to get out of schoolboy habits."

"I'll be glad to help you break them."

"I apologize. Will that do?" Hubie pushed a china figurine aside with his knuckles before setting his brandy down on a polished table. "Now, please, do answer the question. That boy out there is obviously mine."

"Don't be an ass, Hubie."

His cousin pointed his thumb in the air. "I remember Jennie well—very well indeed." He leered. Another finger shot out. "He has the look of a Gerard." Still another finger. "I am apparently quite potent. He isn't my only by-blow." He smiled at this, proud as could be. He held up a fourth finger. "And we all know *you* wouldn't have fathered a child." There was that dangerous light in his eyes again.

"We know nothing of the sort. Ipsial is none of your business," Gerard snapped at the bloody filthy bastard. He must calm himself. His temper would not help stop this danger, only make Hubie aware of his own interest.

"Ipsial. Such an odd name." Hubie picked up his drink, and took a few sips. As he rubbed his knee with his free hand, a slow smile crept over his face. "Ah. Yes. I remember Jennie did not like my first name."

"Neither did you, if I recall correctly. You threatened several younger boys at school—" Gerard began, hoping to head him off.

Hubie interrupted, "But she had a fondness for my middle name, Ishmael. Ipsial, Ishmael. Not precisely the same, but to her uneducated ear, I suppose it would sound similar."

Gerard tried for an amused smile. "I had no notion you had such an imagination, Hubie."

He wanted to get up and pace but knew his cousin would recognize his discomfort. He forced himself to remain in his chair, foot tapping the floor.

Hubie's return grin showed real amusement. "What do you have to say for yourself? You truly want me to believe that a man like you could produce a child?"

176

Gerard would not smash his fist into Hubie's fatuous, knowing smile.

He held his breath rather than speak the anger growing in his gut. What would Miles do? That held the answer. He felt himself relax deep inside and took several long slow breaths.

His smile turned into something more genuine and less like a snarl. Miles would be sympathetic yet stern. He'd treat this spoiled, jumped-up, frustrated cousin with respect but would not allow him to step over any boundaries.

"Hubie, perhaps you might tell me what you really want," he coaxed. "It would save us time."

"Perhaps what I want is my son."

Of course Miles might think that Hubie had the right to the truth, but Gerard wasn't sure he was ready to go that far.

"What do you want that I can give you?" Gerard amended.

"Perhaps if I took him home, I could keep him as some kind of servant."

How in God's name had Hubie seen that Ipsial was important to him, and therefore a possible tool to be used against him? The truth of that fact had only occurred to Gerard in the last few days.

His cousin was probably only fishing for the information. Gerard forced himself to the silent chant of *what would Miles do, what would Miles do*. He'd hide his outrage and fear and turn the subject of conversation back to Hubie.

"Perhaps you might." Gerard forced the words out. "What sort of service would you choose?"

"You disappoint me. You act as if you don't care what happens to the boy."

"I prefer to speak of other topics. You might tell me how your wife is? And your daughter?"

"In need of expensive finery. Womenfolk so often are, unlike most men. But you wouldn't understand that, would you?"

He did understand one thing—Hubie had pushed him all their lives, pushed and pushed until Gerard broke and said something or did something that made him ashamed or that Hubie could use against him.

If Miles were here, he'd look at Hubert with that cool, slightly amused air. Perhaps when someone tried to get him upset, he would plan his trips to Canada or wherever he wanted to hare off to next.

Hubie was saying something, but Gerard wasn't listening. He was realizing how little he wanted to say good-bye to Miles. The abbey needed Miles and so did Ipsial. Hell, he needed Miles too.

"Eve?"

Gerard waited for his own anger at the stupid provocation, but the automatic response did not occur. He understood why that single word had once sent him into a rage. Fear—for of course he didn't want to be seen as different or as less than manly, not when he had been so confused about who he was and how his desires were not growing as they ought. Miles, he thought, could never be a wrong decision.

He raised his eyebrows. "Isn't that joke rather old, Hubie?"

Hubert leaned forward. "I should take that boy, so obviously my son, home with me. Don't you think?"

Calm yourself. He heard Miles's amused voice.

"I thought you had barely enough money to maintain your household."

Hubie licked his lips. Gerard could almost hear the creaking wheels turn as he tried to consider how he'd get the best grip to make Gerard cough up money.

Gerard didn't jump in or grow angry. He only waited.

"If you agree to make me your heir and not that bastard, I will leave him here with you."

Gerard had to laugh. "I will leave the abbey to become a Foundling Asylum rather than make you my heir."

"You have no family feeling. Gerards have lived on this land for centuries."

"I shall leave it to a Gerard. Just not you, Hubie. But peace, cousin. I wish to give you a gift. No, I am not making a poor joke."

The rage in Hubie's eyes turned into avarice. "Whatever this gift might be, it's nothing compared to the abbey."

Gerard wanted to turn the greedy bane of his existence away with nothing and forbid him to come anywhere near the abbey or Ipsial. Yet he recalled how his aunt, Hubie's mother, had been reasonably kind to him during his school holidays. Even as she'd tolerated her younger brother's child, she'd moaned about how she hadn't inherited any part of her beloved childhood home, the abbey. Perhaps her sense of loss had been translated to Hubie and he truly did feel as if the abbey was a family treasure he deserved.

"I hope you know that you and your family may visit any time, provided you give me notice." *So I might run away.* "I am determined to restore the buildings and grounds, so there's no need to mourn the loss of its former glory. Next time you visit, there will be a butler."

Hubie relaxed into his chair. "This gift is to stop me from talking about your unpleasant predilections, of course. Or perhaps it is for the purchase of my bastard."

He is trying to engage you in a fight, he imagined Miles telling him. *For once, do not give in. You show him too much when you do. He is not worth it.* The customary shiver of anger

179

ran through his limbs and then—vanished. Gerard could change and grow. He felt ridiculously glad to be rid of all that fury.

"I don't know what you mean. I am giving you, my cousin, a gift to help you and your family." He sounded so reasonable he almost believed himself. He named a sum that wasn't too outrageous but enough to make Hubie's eyes widen. He added, "Of course I shall help my niece for her coming out when that time arrives."

For a moment, Hubie lost his usual insinuating, baiting air. "Why? Why are you doing this?"

He decided to be honest, or at least as truthful as he could be with Hubie. "I am tired of our unpleasant encounters, Hubert. I wish to live my life without the hostility and fights of our past. I wish to relax."

"You?" Hubie laughed. "You would fight anything that crossed you. You'd box with your own shadow. And if you couldn't beat it down, you'd race it or challenge it to some kind of test. You'd never relax."

Had he been so terrible? No. He probably showed his worst side to Hubie. "After my father died, I rather stopped caring as much. I did not need to win every time." That was more than enough to reveal to the far too interested Hubie. Gerard swallowed the rest of his drink. "I must speak to Mrs. Billings about dinner. You are staying, I expect?"

Hubie smiled. "Yes. Of course I am. Will little Ipsial be eating with us?"

"He doesn't usually eat with me," Gerard lied. "He's in the care of Mr. Kenway, my bailiff."

"That large man who was with him. I wonder why didn't you introduce us?" That light was back in his eyes. So much for Gerard's hope that they might reach a truce.

"Perhaps I should have, but I know you'd rather not pass the time of day with servants."

"He seems like an interesting fellow." Hubie waited, but he wouldn't get a rise from Gerard again. He paused for a long minute before asking, "Have you had a proper dinner since you've been home?"

That was an interesting new tack to embark upon, Gerard thought. It led away from Ipsial and Miles, so he would encourage it. "What do you mean?"

"Surely there must be some quality folk you should entertain. At the very least, you should invite the local clergyman to sup with you, and other worthies he might recommend. Certainly you should uphold the traditions of the abbey's prominence in the area."

If anyone else had made the suggestion, Gerard might think that he made a good point. What could Hubie be scheming now? The imagination boggled. Would he attempt to pick a fight with Gerard? Would he suggest to the local gentry that Gerard had unnatural appetites just to ruin him?

He stifled a sigh. "I expect you're correct, Hubie. But for tonight, we shall be only family."

"The two of us and Ipsial?"

"The two of us."

"Add the boy and his keeper, and I agree."

Gerard couldn't help laughing. "I hadn't known we would need to negotiate the meals, cousin."

"Everything, cousin. We shall see about it *all*."

That was precisely what he'd feared. The money he'd offered, the attempts at peace-making wouldn't be enough. Perhaps he'd send Ipsial and Miles away until he could rid himself of the pest of Hubie. In the meantime, he'd do what he could to keep the situation, and himself, calm.

He felt a surge of pride hours later when Miles and Ipsial made their appearance at the drawing room door per his request. The boy looked neater than he ever had before, so he must have given in to another bath and haircut. Miles did not wear correct dinner attire, but still appeared a gentleman in his dark heather tweed suit.

Of course, Gerard and Hubert had changed for dinner. Gerard had gotten out of the habit of stiff fronts and white tie, as well as the whole soup-and-fish rigmarole of formal meals, but he wouldn't allow Hubie the satisfaction of seeing him less than properly dressed.

They sat at the dining table, and Farley waited on them. He hadn't uttered a word of complaint about being drafted into this role. Gerard wondered if perhaps Mrs. Billings had had a private word with Farley about his unyielding London ways.

"Isn't this pleasant," Hubie said, all condescending joviality.

Ipsial gave him a sideways glance and slurped up more soup. At least he was using a spoon.

"Is Mr. Kenway teaching you, or are you going to a village school, Ipsial?"

The boy looked at Miles, who nodded.

"He's teaching me," Ipsial said.

"And are you a clever child?"

Another look at Miles, another nod. "Mebbe."

Every fatuous question to Ipsial was answered with a look at Miles and a single grudging word or two.

At last Hubie gave up. He turned his attention to Miles, but the topic remained Ipsial. "And you have been in charge of the boy's care how long?"

"Awhile, sir."

"Years? Months?"

Gerard was ready to interrupt the questioning.

Miles pursed his lips, considering. "Depending on how our lessons go, I'd swear it had been centuries. Other times, I'm sure it's been a matter of days. Wouldn't you agree, Ipsial?"

The boy nodded.

Miles had missed a career as diplomat, Gerard thought as he wiped his mouth with a napkin to hide his amusement.

After dinner, Miles excused himself and Ipsial. "The boy should get to bed. I shall take him to my cottage."

"But I sleep..." Ipsial clamped his mouth shut before the words "here" or "just upstairs" came out. Good boy.

"Yes, I know it's early," Miles said. "But come along."

Hubie spoke even before the door was shut behind the bailiff and the boy. "That child has the manners of an oaf. He must have been brought up in a stable yard."

Gerard, who'd been rather proud of how infrequently Ipsial used his fingers in his food, felt the old blinding rage seep in. "You have no right to criticize."

"Why not? He's my get. No, don't bother to deny it."

Gerard glanced at the door, hoping Ipsial was gone. "All right. I won't deny it, then. But consider this. Suppose I threw him at you now, forced you to take him. Would you announce the fact that he's yours to the world?" He waited as Hubie considered his words.

Long seconds of silence ticked past. "I thought not. Ipsial would be nothing more than a weight around your neck. You feign interest in him, but let's suppose you did bring him home with you now. Your wife, your neighbors, your tenants, everyone you know would be appalled."

Gerard had had enough of playacting and pretending not to care about Ipsial. He stood, threw down his napkin and walked close to Hubie.

"Gloves off, cousin. Here is my last word on the subject. Take Ipsial, if you feel you must act as his father." He leaned over Hubie. Familiar anger coursed through him yet transformed—no longer blinding or hot, he felt utterly cold and calm. His voice came out as a harsh whisper. "But if you did anything less than claim Ipsial as your boy, I would know. And if anything happened to him, if he ended up in a workhouse or dead, I would come after you, Hubie. Do you understand? You know I do not back down from a fight. Do not cross me in this. Because if you do, you will regret it for the rest of your life. I would make certain of that. I have no wife, and I do not care as much as you do for reputation. Are you certain you want to risk everything for a boy you don't know or care about just to annoy me?"

Hubie flinched, then pushed back from the table. "I believe I have had enough of this family drama. I think I shall take a stroll around the grounds. Your reputation? Eve, you and your reputation be damned."

Chapter Seventeen

Miles grasped Ipsial's shoulder and steered him away from the dining room door but not before angry raised voices rang out into the hallway. Gerard and Hubert were shouting about the boy's parentage and what should be done with him. One glance down at Ipsial's face told Miles the boy had heard and understood their words.

"Pay no heed," Miles said. "It's just an argument. Your father will sort things out."

"But he's *not* my da, is he? Don't sound like it."

"Perhaps not, but you're his ward nevertheless. He's taken you under his wing." He prayed he was telling the truth. Gerard had not officially adopted Ipsial. He had no real claim on him. And the man was a bit capricious. He might decide all in a moment that he'd rather be in sunny Italy and that Ipsial belonged with the man who'd given him life. Anything was possible.

"Come now. If you're to stay with me tonight, you should gather a few of your things." Miles hurried the boy along the hallway. "I'll wait for you outdoors."

Ipsial silently bounded up the nearest staircase, leaving Miles to stare after the unfortunate lad and wonder how much more upheaval he could take.

It was a relief to leave the stuffy abbey and breathe in great draughts of the cold night air. Miles was never so comfortable as when he was outside. The world made more sense there. It was people, foolish, quarreling, backbiting, meddlesome people, who were exhausting to be around. The stillness of nature soothed his ruffled mood and returned him to a state of calm.

For all of two minutes. Then the loathsome houseguest strode through the door behind him, topcoat on and hat in hand.

Hubert paused on the doorstep while his eyes adjusted to the dim light. His gaze fell on Miles, and he approached him. "The gamekeeper. I'm sorry, I've forgotten your name already."

Amused, Miles wondered which was supposed to be more insulting, that Hubert had forgotten his name or mistaken him for a servant of much lower rank. "I'm Kenway, sir, and I'm the bailiff. We don't have a gamekeeper, as there's no game to speak of on the estate any longer."

"Really? That's a shame, I'd say. The abbey was once a fine, beautiful place. If only my cousin could understand the value of returning the gardens and woods to their former glory."

"We are working hard at restoration, sir."

"But imagine having an entire staff to attend to the many duties that have apparently been foisted on you." Hubert was trying far too hard and too obviously to win Miles's support.

Miles could remain polite, with an effort. "I'm happy with my job as it is."

The man's blue eyes—so very like Gerard's—narrowed, and his friendly manner sloughed off like the snakeskin it was. "Happy with the job, or is it your employer who keeps you so 'happy'?"

No mistaking that sneering suggestion, but Miles pretended not to understand. "Both. I have no complaints, sir," he said mildly. *Hurry, Ipsy. I've had enough of dealing with this fellow.*

As if in response to his inner plea, Ipsial emerged from the house. He stopped and stared at Hubert talking to Miles, then approached slowly, returning to the cautious little creature he'd been when he'd first arrived.

Hubert caught sight of the boy and turned toward him with another of those huge fake smiles he seemed prone to. "There he is. Just the boy I wanted to speak with. Will you walk with me, son?"

Ipsial looked to Miles as he'd done throughout the meal, checking for his approval. This time Miles was not inclined to give it. He frowned his disapproval.

Ipsial planted his feet and folded his arms across his scrawny chest. "What you want?"

"Just to talk to you, my boy, about your future and what being a Gerard means."

"Means I live here," he said brusquely.

"Not necessarily. Not right away, at any rate. There's a good chance you'll go off to school, get some education, learn to be a proper gentleman." Hubert stepped forward and rested a hand on Ipsial's shoulder.

Miles cringed, afraid the boy might bite or kick him in the shins and run off. But Ipsial stood steady as a rock and stared up into his father's eyes. "You want to take me away."

"I think it might be for the best." Hubert bent over to level his gaze with Ipsial's, and this time Miles felt an unreasonable fear that Cousin Hubie might be the one doing the biting. He looked like a predator about to strike. "This place is not good for a child, too isolated and populated with unsavory influences. Your second cousin Everett is not a good caregiver for a young boy. Not at all."

"He wants me to go with you," Ipsial said, erasing any doubt that he'd overheard Gerard's raised voice.

"Your mother would have wanted you to be with me. She

sent you to the abbey because I'd mentioned it was the Gerard family home. She must have thought I'd be there to welcome you, that your *true* father would live there."

"Enough," Miles interrupted, moving toward the frozen tableau of father and son. But what could he do? Drag Ipsial away, or thrash Hubert for telling the truth?

"You're my dad, then," Ipsial said coolly.

"I believe I am...son, and together we're going to make sure that the abbey is here for you when you're a grown man."

Miles was confused about what angle slippery Hubert was playing. At first it seemed he'd merely wanted to take a share of the money after Gerard sold the property. But after learning of Ipsial's existence, he apparently thought he could somehow maneuver his way into owning the entire estate through his bastard son. How he thought claiming paternity would accomplish that, Miles wasn't sure. One thing he was sure about was that it was time to get Ipsial away from this man.

"Come along, Ipsial," Miles ordered. "It's late. You should bid good night to Mr. Gerard."

Hubert straightened. "Nonsense. Let the boy walk and talk with me a little while. We've lost far too much time already. I have the right to get to know my son."

Every fiber of Miles's being screamed "no", but he had no actual right to keep Hubert away from Ipsial. His diplomatic attempt at separating them had failed, and now Ipsial, rather than shying away from the stranger, appeared ready to accompany him.

"'S all right, Mr. Kenway," he said, suddenly sounding more mature than Miles had ever heard him. "I'll be along soon."

With Hubert's hand on the boy's shoulder, the pair walked off down a flagstone path, leaving Miles frustrated and helpless. Perhaps Gerard was wrong about his cousin. Certainly the man coveted the abbey, but maybe he could also be a good guardian to Ipsial. Besides which, neither Miles nor Gerard had any inherent right to Ipsial. Hubert Gerard *was* the boy's father.

Knowing this and feeling it were two different things. Miles stood in indecision for mere moments before trailing after the pair, skulking in the shadows at a distance where he could still hear their conversation.

"Just a turn around the garden. It's too dark to go too far from the house," Hubert said as they walked down a pathway. "I am quite distraught to learn of your mother's death. When did it happen?"

Ipsial's shoulders rose and fell in a shrug. "A while ago."

"And you made your way here all alone? What a brave lad." Hubert's voice was as greasy as a stove. "Mr. Kenway has been taking care of you, and then my cousin Everett arrived and offered to be your father. Is that correct?"

"Yeah." Ipsial's shoes audibly scuffed over the ground.

"It seems you've grown to admire Mr. Kenway and Mr. Gerard. Is that true?"

"Yeah."

"Have you ever noticed them behaving...in a way that's unusual for two men? Have you ever seen them touch each another?"

Miles caught his breath as he realized the trap Hubert was laying. He hoped to use the boy as a witness to discredit his cousin and lay claim to the abbey, or to blackmail Gerard for a large sum.

"Sure," was Ipsial's laconic answer.

"You mean you've seen them touch?"

"First night here, Mr. Gerard and Mr. Kenway came to blows."

"Oh. Well, that's strange. A gentleman is set upon by his bailiff and yet keeps him in his employ? Are you certain you didn't see them do anything besides fight? Maybe they were wrestling on the ground together, thrashing around and grunting in a...a playful way. Is that what you saw?"

"I saw Mr. Kenway punch Mr. Gerard in the jaw. A good 'un, too. Snapped his head right around. That what you mean?"

Miles smiled. He recognized Ipsial's dry tone. It sounded exactly like Gerard's. The boy knew perfectly well what he'd seen that night—men kissing. He was feigning ignorance for Hubert's benefit. No. Not for Hubert's, but for Miles and Gerard. The boy was protecting them. Miles's heart swelled with affection for the child he'd once thought was a lost cause.

The boy's answer seemed to take the wind from Hubert's sails, but he gamely tried another tack. "I'm certain these two men you're so fond of have shown you great affection. Are there any instances you can remember where one of them touched you—something beyond a pat on the head?"

White-hot rage blistered through Miles at the insinuation that either of them might have interfered with Ipsial. He was seconds away from charging out of the shadow of a tree like some wild bull and goring the despicable Hubert Gerard. But he maintained his calm and listened as Ipsial once again neatly turned the tables on his questioner.

"Had to go in the tub once, and Mr. Kenway and Mrs. Billings scrubbed my neck something fierce. I hate baths. If I went with you, would I get to stop taking 'em?"

Miles had no doubt that clever Ipsial was toying with the man like a cat with a mouse as the boy pressed on. "And would you let me shoot your rifle? Mr. Kenway taught me how to shoot and how to use a knife to skin things."

Miles had never heard the boy lie so fluently. He felt

appalled and proud.

"I'm really good with a knife and so quiet I can sneak up on rabbits and catch them in a snare. Do you live where there's animals to kill?"

"No. My home is in the city."

"Too bad. I like to kill things."

"At any rate, a young man of your age should be off at boarding school, meeting chums his own age and learning how to be a gentleman. I'm sure you'd do well in the classroom, a bright lad like you."

Hubert seemed to have caught on to the fact that Ipsial was vaguely threatening him and so offered to cage him with headmasters and vicious peers. Touché.

Ipsial suddenly abandoned all pretense. "Mr. Gerard may not want me here no more. But I'm not goin' anywhere with *you*." With that abrupt statement, he turned and ran off into the darkness, leaving Hubert staring after him.

Miles continued to stand completely still in the shadow of a tree so as not to attract Hubert's attention. The man shook his head and cursed under his breath, then stalked back to the house with a stiff-legged, angry stride. Only after the door closed behind him did Miles emerge from his hiding spot.

It was a fair bet he'd find Ipsial waiting for him at home, so Miles trudged across the formal grounds and into the woods. But when he reached his cottage, no lights were lit and no fire burned on the hearth. Ipsial wasn't there.

"Little bugger's gone to ground again," Miles muttered as he laid a fire. He was torn about whether to go to the tumbledown cottage where the boy had previously made his nest or wait until morning. Knowing Ipsial's nature, the boy wanted to be alone to think. He would come to Miles when he was ready and not before. Perhaps he would show up yet tonight. Miles made a comfortable pallet in front of the hearth just in case. He would be patient and wait for the little bird to come home to roost.

As he stretched out to sleep, his thoughts milled nervously as horses before an impending storm. Hubert Gerard was a wildcard thrown unexpectedly into the game. The man was determined to strong-arm Gerard into giving him something— money or land, it didn't seem to matter which, but did he have the power to pressure Gerard into capitulating? Would he go to the extreme of legally claiming Ipsial just to spite his cousin? And would he dare besmirch the family name by smearing Everett's name with a rumor of perversion?

That would do less harm to Miles than to Gerard. Miles would suffer, of course, but eventually he could simply pack his bags and board a ship. This thought depressed his spirit rather than raised it. His usual restlessness had abandoned him of late. And if he should leave, what would happen to Ipsial?

Tossing and turning with sleep just beyond his reach, Miles fought the urge to throw off his covers and go to Gerard right now, wake him up and talk about what would happen next. But his late night presence in the house would only give Hubert fresh fodder to feed his story of scandal. No. He would wait until morning and then catch Gerard at the first opportunity.

He returned to his mental list of destinations, wondering if any of them would appeal to him again.

Chapter Eighteen

After a nearly sleepless night, Gerard woke to the knowledge that Halfwit Hubie, that perennial thorn in his side, was back in his life, wreaking havoc in a new and more sinister way. Being taunted or beaten in his school days didn't compare to what his cousin could do to him now. That was the trouble with coming to care for a person—they could be used as a threat against one. The mere thought of Ipsial being snatched away from him was intolerable. He'd grown exceedingly fond of the boy.

But what could Hubert do, really? He could hardly prove his paternity, and would he really bring scandal on his own head just to cross Everett?

Hubie's threat to claim Ipsial was more of a game move than an actual likelihood. If worse came to worst, Gerard could swear he'd had relations with Jennie McCray himself and that he was certain Ipsial was his son.

That idea cheered him greatly and moved him out of bed and into his clothes. He'd grown used to country hours. Perhaps he could leave and return before Hubie woke to discover him gone.

His first order of business today would be to find Ipsial and reassure the boy of his place in this house. The clever boy had likely caught wind that he was a bone of contention between the cousins. He would also have a chance to talk with Miles and remind him that they must be extra circumspect during Hubert's visit. Of course, just the idea of seeing Miles made

Gerard want to be anything *but* circumspect. Since their first few encounters, they'd had no time at all together.

But all that would have to wait until Hubie was gone and Ipsial was safe. Whatever amount of money he had to pay Hubert to get rid of him would be worth it—if only he could be certain that money would accomplish the task.

Gerard ate a light, hurried breakfast of toast and tea, then slipped out the refectory door. The world lay poised between rainfalls. Water still occasionally pattered from leaves, and the gray skies promised more. They'd probably never see full sun today. He could see his breath in the chilled, damp air. He buried his hands in his jacket pockets and set off for Miles's cottage.

He found Miles pulling on his heavy canvas jacket, just preparing to leave.

"Is he with you?" Miles asked.

"Hubie? No. He's asleep."

Miles ran his fingers through his disheveled hair. He'd probably not combed it this morning. "I mean Ipsial. He didn't return to me. I hoped he'd gone back to the main house. He was rather upset."

"He's not at the abbey." Gerard fisted his hands in his pockets rather than reach out and smooth an errant lock of Miles's hair. "What upset the boy? Ah, no. I can guess. My conversation with Hubie? He overheard it, didn't he?"

"Yes, that upset him. Among other things." Miles grabbed his hat and shoved it onto his head. "I suppose we ought to go find Ipsial."

"Of course we should. Why wouldn't we?" Gerard supposed he sounded unreasonably irritable, but he couldn't do anything about the pestilential Hubie or the fact that their boy had been hurt by the bounder.

194

Their boy, he thought. That was fanciful notion on his part. He grew even more irritated.

Miles remained unruffled, of course. "He might need some time alone. Come, Gerard. He is no delicate child to be injured by simple words."

"He might be. We all might be," Gerard grumbled. He followed Miles.

Miles led the way toward the woods. "He must have gone to ground in his old haunt."

Gerard's steps slowed, and his heart beat faster at the prospect of entering the abandoned hut again. *You've been there more than once lately,* he scolded himself. *Stop with your theatrics.*

But his body did not heed him, and the shivering began as they drew closer to the hut. The ice coursed through his veins, his intestines turned to water, his heart tried to leap from his body. He was going to be sick. He drove his fingernails into his palm to stop himself as he began to breathe too hard and fast.

"A moment," he called to Miles, trying to sound unconcerned. He stumbled into the soaked underbrush and deposited his breakfast there. An empty stomach must help improve things, he thought as he wiped his mouth with his hand.

He backed away and almost bumped into Miles, who grabbed him by the shoulders, turned him around and embraced him. Warm, strong arms immediately brought Gerard to a better world, and his own strength slowly filled him.

Miles sighed. "I had no notion you were ill. Return to the abbey, and I'll look for Ipsial."

Gerard laid his head against the cold, wet canvas of Miles's coat, the trembling in his limbs relaxing. "It's the cottage." He reluctantly pulled away from Miles's hug and said in a cracked voice, "I'm not ill. We must find Ipsial."

Miles clutched his arm to prevent him walking away. "The cottage? What do you mean?"

Gerard tasted something horrid in his mouth and spat. "Ipsial..." he tried again.

"All right, we'll keep looking. We'll walk. And you will tell me what you meant." His unwavering stare focused on Gerard. "You are pale and you still are shaking. If you're not ill, you're afraid."

Gerard waited for the surge of anger, the desperate need to fight. Perhaps he was too worried about Ipsial or his body had had enough, because he remained calm. "All right," he agreed and strode toward the gardener's hut.

"Why are you afraid of the place?" Miles asked again.

Gerard wanted to get this over with. He broke into a trot. "When I was a boy, my mother was rarely here. I don't recall her well. Except that last day. That I remember. That..." He had never said these words aloud. His father's devastated face, his hushed whispers. *"Do not tell. Do not tell anyone."*

"I came to the hut and found my mother and another man. Someone I did not know. Both were dead. He was shot. I think she'd been strangled, for her face was purple. And there was so much blood and bits of gray muck. Even then I knew it was brain matter."

The words rushed out of him. "They had almost no clothes, and they lay on the floor, the dirt-and-stone floor of the gardener's hut. I couldn't understand why they had so few clothes. I thought it's too chilly to be here without clothes. And that blood—I walked close enough so that my shoes got blood on them."

He slowed because he was out of breath again. Too much talking, not enough inhaling. "The blood remained on my shoes,

196

and that's how I could remember the whole thing. My father ordered me to forget. He took me back to my room, told the servants I was ill. They put me to bed.

"He must have buried my mother's body on his own. The man was discovered later, alone. But my father hid my mother. I thought of him whenever I felt weak. I spent so little time, only a matter of minutes, near those bodies. He must have been with them for hours. And he never showed any weakness."

He dragged in a long breath, and words and air seemed to come more easily. "I tried to speak of it to him later. He slapped me and reminded me that I wasn't to ever mention the matter.

"'Even with you?' I asked him and he nodded."

Gerard squeezed his eyes shut. He lowered his voice. "I had to know, so I asked him another time if he'd killed them. Her." He swallowed back the familiar rise of nausea. "He gave me such a look, pure venom, and said, 'Of course not, you fool. I would never do such a thing. I expect he killed her and then himself.' I believed him."

Miles made a small sympathetic sound and reached out to touch his arm. "'Tis an awful thing you witnessed. No wonder you could hardly face this place again." He paused, then added, "But do you really believe those are the true facts of what happened that night?"

He laughed without humor. "It was not that my father was incapable of lying. On the contrary, he did a wonderful job for the rest of his life. No one here thought he lied when he said Mama went to London. No one here or in London suspected he didn't tell the truth when he said she'd died of influenza."

"And you are sure your father didn't murder them?" Miles's voice was quiet, gentle, but matter-of-fact—without a trace of pity, thank God.

For the first time in long minutes, Gerard felt the nausea

recede. His heart slowed. "I suppose I don't know and never will. But I believe him, because in truth, it was not in his nature to act with such passion. My father was a tidy, methodical man, a man who didn't like fusses. He wouldn't resort to such a bloody mess. He would ignore my mother's indiscretions. Perhaps he always had." He shuddered. "And I recall a gun next to the dead man's body. Next to his hand. Mr. Hughes had a violent temper, people in London said. He'd lost his job as a banker because of it. My theory is that he must have followed my mother when she tried to return to the abbey and my father and killed her before she could."

"Did you father tell you the rest of it? About Mr. Hughes?"

"No. Of course not. My father and I never spoke of the matter. Nor did he even mention the man's name. I hired an inquiry agent in London recently, two agents, actually, Marsh and Court." He smiled briefly at the memory. "For some reason, I suspect those two were more than simply partners in the agency."

Miles opened the door to the cottage, calling, "Ipsial? Are you here?"

Silence met them. Miles strode over to the fireplace—right across the spot where Gerard's mother and her lover had once lain—and put his hand near the ashes. "The hearth is cold. I'm almost certain he didn't spend the night here."

Gerard's mind snapped back to the present and the task at hand. "Well, unless he's hiding someplace in the house, where do you think he might be?"

Miles shook his head. "He could've set up camp any place on the grounds."

"In the rain with no shelter? A city child like that? Has he done such a thing before?"

Miles thought for a moment. "No. I don't think so."

Worry wove into the first frissons of anger in Gerard. "I wish you'd have informed me last night that he'd disappeared. We could have begun the search for him then."

"I didn't know, and at any rate, I wouldn't worry quite yet. Ipsy has a way of coming and going like a cat. He'll likely show up again around the next mealtime. In fact, I wouldn't be surprised if he were getting his breakfast from Mrs. Billings right now."

Gerard clicked his tongue in irritation. "What exactly did you and he overhear in the hallway? Does he know that Hubert is his true father? Don't you think that might upset the lad?"

Miles slapped his cap against the side of his leg, and droplets of water sprayed from it. His expression betrayed uncertainty as his mouth thinned in a grim line. "Truth be told, Ipsial *did* seem quite angry last time I saw him. He talked with your cousin in the garden, and I listened in on the conversation. Hubert admitted he was Ipsial's father and tried to convince him to go away with him, and he..."

"What? What else happened in this conversation you've waited till now to share with me?" Gerard's temper was rising fast and fiery now.

Miles sighed. "Hubert tried to get Ipsial to admit to having witnessed us together. He was searching for ammunition to use against you. I don't know what your cousin plans, but it's clear he wants control over the abbey, and in order to get that, he must have a way to threaten you."

"I see. And what did Ipsial reveal to him?" A hunk of lead had taken up residence in the pit of Gerard's stomach. "Come outside. We will keep looking."

They stepped out of the dank cottage, but Gerard barely noticed they'd left the evil place. He was filled with dread for the little wretch, and he was unused to strong worry for anyone.

Miles laid a hand on his shoulder. "Ipsial revealed nothing. Nothing at all. The boy remained quiet about what he may or may not have seen of us together." Miles grimaced. "And the last thing he said to Hubert before he ran away was that he would never go with him—even if you didn't want him here any longer."

"What?" Gerard's shout frightened several birds in the nearby bush, and they shot out into the air. "Why would he think I wouldn't want him? And why did you not think it was important to inform me of all this immediately?"

Miles frowned and stared into his eyes, his big hand still resting on his shoulder. "Because I know Ipsial. He's a loner at heart. It was the dead of night, and I didn't imagine he'd actually go anywhere. I was almost certain he'd decided to sleep here. And, as I said, he might be at breakfast right now. We should walk back to the abbey and check."

Gerard's pulse beat in his ears deafeningly. His outrage was far out of proportion to the annoyance he should feel toward Miles right now. He recognized that, yet he couldn't seem to control the anger that had taken hold of him. All he knew right now was that he must find Ipsial and see that he was safe. No pretend son of his was going to go through life feeling unwanted or unloved.

Without another word to Miles, Gerard turned and strode out of the clearing. All the way back to the house, he felt Miles's presence behind him, heard the heavy tread of his boots and wanted to apologize for his anger. But why should he, when Kenway was in the wrong? He let that tide of righteous anger carry him all the way home, and when he entered the breakfast room and encountered Hubert calmly eating smoked kippers and eggs, he unleashed his fury on his cousin.

"I am well used to your behavior, but it stops now. How

dare you come into my home and harass and intimidate my son? Despite what you believe, Ipsial is *not* yours. Do you think you're the only man who has known Jennie McCray's favors? I didn't say anything last night, but now I'm letting you know in no uncertain terms that Ipsial is my son. Sprung from my loins. Heir to my estate and my name, and I will legally claim him as such. Do you really want to fight me about this? Would you stake your reputation and risk society's censure just to undermine me? I think not."

Gerard listened to these words pour out of him in a torrent as if a stranger had taken hold of his body and spoke through him. The look of shock on Hubert's red face was priceless, and Gerard saw the moment when his cousin's will broke and he accepted defeat. Hubie turned his gaze away, blinked, looked down at the floor. His shoulders hunched.

Gerard's temper had flared and now faded, but he would not back down. "I will pay you a reasonable sum for your perceived 'share' of the family estate, and then we will speak no more of it. I don't withdraw my offer to assist your daughter's debut, but do not expect a ha'penny more. Am I understood?"

Hubie nodded dumbly, his hands still welded to his knife and fork, which were poised over his plate full of fish.

Ah, a little blind rage could do a body good. Gerard was trembling slightly from the strength of his emotion, but he felt good. He allowed himself a heartbeat to enjoy the sensation of victory, but more pressing matters summoned him.

He went to the bell and tugged it. Mrs. Billings appeared soon after.

"Please summon the staff, Mr. Farley included. We'll be conducting a search for Ipsial. My son is missing."

Her brows shot up, her mouth opened, but she didn't speak. After a long moment, she said, "Yes, sir. Right away. Do you have instructions on where we might look for him?"

Gerard turned to Miles. "You know the property and Ipsial best, Mr. Kenway. Where should we search?"

Miles gave him a half smile, then turned his attention to Mrs. Billings. "Tell Joey and the others to concentrate on the north end of the property, beyond the stables. I'll go to the village."

"You can't find the boy?" Cousin Hubie asked. He'd put down his knife and fork at last.

"Yes."

"He's a handful."

Gerard strode from the room before he lost his temper again.

Hubie called after him, "No insult intended, cousin. Just a lively young chap."

"That's certainly true," Miles muttered. "Boy's a nuisance."

Gerard felt himself smile. "A young idiot."

"Indeed."

"I only hope he's safe."

"He's resourceful and intelligent. Much like his father."

Gerard paused, his hand on the handle of the door to the courtyard. "No need to pretend now that we're alone again. That infernal Hubie is his father."

"That's where you're wrong, Gerard. You are. I heard the truth of it in your voice, and I've seen it in your actions lately. You weren't lying. Ipsial is your son."

Gerard had to swallow twice before he could answer. "Thank you. Shall we find him and remind him of the fact?"

Chapter Nineteen

Gerard's long stride covered the gravel path quickly. Miles ducked under a wrought iron trellis and followed. He half hoped the man would lash out again. Poor Gerard seemed so tense, he must break or release his fury.

Miles wished he could ease Gerard's weight of emotion. For a short time in the gardener's cottage, he'd seemed to at last stop hiding the burden and share it with Miles.

The story Gerard told of discovering his mother's body would make anyone's blood cold. How could he have kept such a secret to himself all this time? And despite what he said about his father's innocence, he must wonder if his father had killed his mother and her lover.

Gerard walked so quickly, Miles had to run to catch up. "You're fast," he said as he jogged along beside him.

"I'm in a hurry." Gerard bowed his head against a sudden rush of wind.

"We'll find Ipsial," Miles said as they started down the hill to the village. "He has always returned. And that was before you had tamed him."

Gerard stopped and turned to him. "I'm sorry I lost my temper with you, Miles."

"I don't mind." The funny thing was he didn't mind, perhaps because he could see the pain behind the temper.

"I do." Gerard's mouth twisted into a rueful grin. "What's more, I'll try not to do it again, but I make no guarantees."

"Best not." Miles laughed.

They began walking again, Miles stopping to peer into the damp underbrush every now and again. He hoped the boy was smart enough to stay inside on a dreary day like this. A pity he and Gerard weren't that sensible.

They called his name when they stopped to look, but without much conviction. The boy would be tucked into a nice warm place, Miles hoped. Ipsial would reappear, surly and whey-faced, and it would take all of their coaxing to get him to speak to them easily again.

"You have such a grim expression. I hope you're not thinking about leaving my service," Gerard said. He might have been joking, but Miles treated the question as if it was an honest inquiry. He had a simple answer for that.

"No. I like my work. I like you and your son. I am happy here."

Gerard got that wide-eyed, openmouthed look again. For such a strong man, his moments of astonishment were funny, echoing Ipsial at his most charming.

"Thank you for that," he said again, softly. "It helps to... It helps."

They walked in silence for a time.

"In truth, I'm usually a restless man," Miles said. He'd seen Gerard's flaws, and he felt he must admit his own.

"I noticed you don't stay at a job long. A year or so at your past postings. It should have stopped me hiring you."

"Why did you decide to hire me?"

Gerard chuckled. "Your trustworthy face? Your shoulders? They seemed broad enough for the job."

Was he making a lewd remark? Perhaps yes, judging from the smile lingering on his lips.

Miles said, "You trusted me and yet it took a great deal of effort to drag you to the abbey, Mr. Gerard. Several letters, in fact."

"I was a fool. I should have followed you north almost immediately after you left my lawyer's office." His smile widened. "After all, I watched you leave too. The view was inspiring."

"How pleasant to learn I was hired for my shoulders and, er, other attributes," Miles said.

"No need to scowl. In truth you were hired because you seemed intelligent and honest." Gerard still wore that broad smile, however.

They arrived at the first houses of the village and walked more slowly.

"Where should we go first?" Miles asked.

"To the Goat and Grape, I think. Mr. Reynolds is a fine source of information."

Miles winced. "Indeed he is. We should consider which sort of stories we want broadcast to the villagers."

"The bare facts, within reason. Hubert Gerard is visiting the abbey. We are here at the village because Ipsial, who is *my* son, is missing. They can speculate about anything else."

"Let us hope they don't," Miles murmured.

Gerard clapped his hand to the middle of Miles's back. "We will survive this."

We? Did he mean the two of them as individuals? Or were the two of them together something more? Miles had never fancied himself as part of a unit, beyond his immediate family.

"Very well." He settled his cap on his head and followed his employer into the smoky public room of the Goat and Grapes.

Mr. Reynolds had already taken his place by the fire today.

He pushed himself up from the chair in greeting, then dropped back onto the seat.

"Good morning, gentlemen," he called. "Dreary weather we're having, eh, sir?"

They joined him by the fire. Miles put his cap down on a table and held his reddened hands up near the flames while he rubbed the chill from his fingers.

Mr. Reynolds tapped his pipe against the stone side of the fireplace. "I hear tell Mr. Hubert Gerard is visiting the abbey. Haven't seen him in quite a time. I recall his mother, your aunt, of course. She was a nervous girl. Very nervous."

Miles wondered if the Home Secretary could use a talent like Mr. Reynolds. He was a marvel when it came to gathering and disseminating information.

"Yes, my cousin is visiting." Gerard's smile didn't reach his eyes, but perhaps no one but Miles would notice.

Mr. Reynolds waved a thick-knuckled hand at the chairs set up near him. "Care to take a seat, Mr. Gerard? Mr. Kenway?" He pulled out a tin of tobacco. "I'd be glad to stand you a drink, sir, and catch up on the latest news from the abbey."

"We would enjoy the opportunity, except we're rather in a hurry. We're looking for Master Ipsial and only stopped in here to find out if anyone has seen him."

Mr. Reynolds, who'd been packing tobacco into his pipe, stopped and examined him. "Master Ipsial? You mean that boy what came in here with you before?"

"Yes." Gerard cleared his throat. "Ipsial Gerard, my son." He said the words loud enough so the five people in the room would hear. Possibly anyone in the private parlor might hear as well.

Silence fell, and only the pop and sizzle of the fire interrupted it. That settled the matter, Miles thought with some satisfaction. Gerard might as well take out an advertisement in the *Times*.

Gerard looked around the room at each of the men who looked back at him with avid interest. "If anyone should see Master Ipsial, please tell him to return home to the abbey. We are worried about him."

"Certainly, sir," said the barmaid. "We'll spread the word too."

"Yes, I was hoping you might." Gerard walked over and laid several coins on the bar. "Good morning, all."

They left the inn, and Miles wished he could seize Gerard and dance him about for a few steps. "Well done, Gerard," he said. "I wasn't sure you would carry through."

"I never back down from a challenge."

"I hadn't challenged you."

"No. Ipsial did." Gerard turned his face up to the sky. "The rain has stopped again for the moment, thank goodness."

"Where shall we look next?"

Gerard smiled. "We should visit Greenwood's. Ipsial seemed quite taken by the village shop when we visited."

They strolled down the street. Perhaps the end of the rain or the moment in the inn had calmed Gerard. He even hummed under his breath as they walked.

"Hubie will leave today, I think," he said. "If he doesn't take the idea into his own head, I will help him arrive at that decision."

Miles snorted.

"I expect your sister will arrive very soon."

"Next week," Miles confirmed.

"It will be good," Gerard said softly as if to himself. "The future, here with you, if you stay. It will be bright, don't you think?"

He wasn't talking to himself. His quiet words were for Miles.

Miles didn't dare look at him in case his smile revealed too much to anyone looking out a window or passing by. He directed his wide grin at a window box of mums, but his words were only for Gerard. "Yes. I wouldn't miss it for the world."

He'd be giving up the world, of course, but he barely minded the fact. The trains and boats would have to travel without him.

When he entered Greenwood's store, the mingled odors of apples, tobacco, shoe leather and starch from bolts of fabric filled Gerard's senses. Living the city life, he'd grown used to stores that catered to a particular item, but here farming tools fought for space with starched collars. The bright-colored candy in jars caught his attention as he knew they would Ipsial's. He had the odd sensation of retracing the boy's footsteps as he approached the counter.

"Mr. Gerard! May I help you, sir?" The shopkeeper emerged from a back room, chewing what was likely a bite of breakfast— or perhaps an early lunch, as midday was fast approaching.

"Mr. Greenwood, have you seen the boy I brought here several weeks ago? I'm afraid he's suffered a bit of a childish temper and has run off. I thought he might have been beckoned here by images of sweets dancing in his head."

Creases framed the elderly man's broad smile. "Indeed, you guessed right, sir." He jerked his head toward the open door behind him. "Lad just had a bit of something to eat, and I was convincing him to return home."

"Very good." Relief flooded Gerard, his tense muscles loosening all at once so he nearly felt the need to collapse into a chair. Of course, he hadn't really believed Ipsial had gone too far, but the thought of what the boy had overheard—those words about giving him to Hubert as if the boy were no more than a parcel to be passed around—had been repeating over and over in Gerard's mind. Poor Ipsial wouldn't have understood that he was merely making a point to his cousin. He would only have heard the part about not being wanted.

Greenwood beckoned Gerard and Miles over and shuffled a little closer. "The boy asked me for work. Wanted to sweep the floors and dust the shelves." He chuckled. "I imagine he pictured himself keeping the candy jars well organized for me. Never you fear, sir, he's not the first little lad who has taken to the road in anger at his parents. Go speak to him."

"Thank you, Mr. Greenwood." Gerard shot a glance at Miles before starting around the counter.

"Maybe this time you should talk privately with the boy," Miles said quietly enough that the old man couldn't hear. "I'll stay here."

Gerard realized he was right. This was a matter between father and son. Miles had already established a strong bond with the child, but Gerard was the one who must convince Ipsial he wanted him to be a part of his life.

He headed toward the doorway to the dimly lit back room, feeling as nervous as a cat in a room full of bulldogs. He prayed he'd find the right words to soothe Ipsial's hurt feelings.

His eyes adjusted to the gloom, focusing on a small table, a pair of wooden stools, a couple of mugs and plates strewn with crumbs, but no little boy. He heard the back door creak close and cursed. Ipsial had hared off again.

Gerard ran after him, blundering through the crowded little

room, knocking his hip sharply into the corner of the table and nearly sending it toppling. He pushed open the rear door of the shop, which led into a narrow, smelly alleyway, just in time to glimpse Ipsial running around the corner.

"Ipsial, stop!" he called as he raced to catch up. He turned the corner right on the boy's heels and clapped a hand on his shoulder. "Stop running. Listen to me."

Ipsial wheeled around and kicked him smartly in the shin. The blow made him wince, but Gerard didn't let go. He grasped Ipsial's narrow shoulder tightly and pulled him closer.

Ipsial punched his stomach. Despite several layers of coat, waistcoat and shirt, the punch was hard enough to drive the breath from him. "Lemme go. I won't let you give me to him. I won't go."

Gerard used his most commanding voice and a squeeze of his fingers to try to still the boy. "I'm not giving you to anyone. Please stop hitting and listen to me."

Ipsial looked up at him with eyes so wild and a scowl so fierce Gerard almost feared the boy would lunge at him again. Gerard held that angry blue gaze with his own. "Listen to me," he repeated. "You misunderstood what you heard last night."

"No, I didn't. That man is my real father, not you. But I won't go with him. I can tell how mean he is. I won't get pasted no more."

Gerard ached at the rasping words that seemed torn from Ipsial's throat. "No you won't. Trust me, I never truly intended to let you go live with Hubert, even if he is your actual father. I know the man too well, and while I don't believe he'd beat you, I also don't think he'd be kind. No, Ipsial, you *must* stay with me and with Mr. Kenway. That's decided." He said all this in a rush before Ipsial could squirm away again.

Now both his hands clasped Ipsial's shoulders, and he bent

so their eyes were on a level. "Do you hear me? The abbey is your home, now and forever. I am adopting you as my son, and there will be no doubt in anyone's mind to whom you belong."

Ipsial studied his face, eyes shifting back and forth as if reading a book and trying to decide if the words read were true or not.

"You can trust me," Gerard told him. "And I'll have no more running away from you, my boy, no matter how angry—or scared—you might sometimes be. Let me tell you a secret. I've fought my fears and my temper my entire life, so I know how difficult that fight can be. I will help you grow past your fears and learn to control your temper. That's what a father does for his son."

Gerard managed a tiny smile while suppressing the prickle of tears his declaration brought to his eyes. Seemed he was overly emotional ever since returning to the abbey.

Ipsial continued to study him intently but less doubtfully. "Yeah?"

"Yes," Gerard promised. "So, are you ready to go home now?"

"Will you send that cousin away?"

"As soon as possible."

"And where's Mr. Kenway?"

"Waiting for us inside." Gerard had loosened his grip once Ipsial stopped squirming, and now he put a hand on the boy's back and steered him into the shop.

Before they left the rear room to enter the store, Ipsial stopped walking. Gerard looked down at him, waiting patiently for whatever the boy needed to say.

"I got one question."

"All right. You can feel free to ask me anything anytime,

Ipsial."

"Will we finally go riding like you promised?"

Having expected a weightier question, Gerard laughed. Trust Ipsial to focus on what *he* considered the vital questions in his life. "Yes, I expect we will, many times. You shall become quite the horseman, and Miles will teach you how to hunt if you wish."

Ipsial considered. "I like shooting. I wouldn't mind. Though I don't s'pose I'd like dead animals much."

"No," Gerard agreed. "Dead creatures can be very unpleasant unless they're on a dinner plate. Perhaps you could shoot at targets instead."

Ipsial nodded. "All right. Targets are good."

Together they entered the shop, where Miles awaited them, an expectant expression lifting his brows. When Gerard smiled at him, he nodded slightly; then he spoke gruffly to Ipsial. "You ready to go home, lad?"

A flash of brilliance lit Ipsial's bony face as a grin came and went quick as lightning. "Yeah."

212

Chapter Twenty

Gerard dreaded having to confront Hubie once more when he returned to the house. He'd told Miles to keep Ipsial with him for the afternoon, distracting him with chores until Gerard could pry Hubie out of the house. But in the end, ousting his unwanted guest proved quite easy.

Gerard met Hubert in the library where he was halfway through a bottle of brandy and offered him the cheque he had filled out. "As discussed," he said succinctly.

Hubert took the paper and stared blearily at the writing; then he tucked it into his waistcoat pocket before taking another sip of his drink.

"I must ask you to take your leave now. I've told the servants you'll be leaving in an hour. The carriage will be ready to convey you to the station then. You have a first-class return, I imagine?"

Hubert's eyebrows shot up. "What, today?"

"The train for London leaves in an hour and a half."

The drunken man opened his mouth as if about to protest but released a belch instead. He took another glance at Gerard's glowering countenance, then rose unsteadily to his feet and walked from the room without another word.

Gerard almost felt inclined to follow and make sure Hubie was really clearing out, but he waited, fidgeting with papers on his desk, which he could barely focus on until he heard the distant sound of a carriage driving away. Only then did he leave the library.

After a restless night and an emotion-filled day, he thought he'd like nothing better than to have a lie-down until suppertime. Ipsial was safe with Miles, and that would be soon enough to tell him that Hubert was gone. But as he neared his bedchamber, Gerard heard voices from within and paused in the hallway. A man and a woman. He recognized his valet's voice and...could that possibly be Mrs. Billings talking with him?

Her normally strident voice cooed like a mourning dove, soft and low. The heavier tone of Farley's voice was a sleepy undercurrent to her quiet murmuring.

Gerard stood in shocked bemusement, because there was no mistaking the seductive tones of the stiff-necked valet and overbearing housekeeper. "Mother of God!" he muttered before backing away from the closed bedroom door.

Inconceivable that two such proper persons would not only indulge in an illicit liaison but use the master's very bedchamber for their meeting. He couldn't have been more amazed if toads had fallen from the skies or gold had cascaded from a rainbow. Both were equally outrageous images to view with the frightening thought of nude middle-aged servants cavorting in his bed.

Just then the door opened, and the pair emerged, still intimately talking and chuckling. Before he could dodge down a different corridor, Farley and Billings spotted him, and stopped and stared slack-jawed.

"Sir, I imagined you'd be seeing off Mr. Hubert Gerard." Farley was as close to flustered as Gerard had ever heard him.

"He's already gone." Gerard's gaze darted back and forth between his disheveled manservant and the matron of the house. He felt his cheeks burning to rival their reddened faces. "I, uh, thought I might rest before dinner, but instead I think

I'll... Yes, I'll take a stroll around the garden." He turned on his heel and fled.

Thus Gerard found himself driven from the abbey and walking across the grounds, his feet turning of their own accord away from the gardens and toward the pasture where he knew Miles and Ipsial were working on rebuilding the stone wall.

He saw their two beloved figures across a field of golden-brown grass undulating in waves in the breeze. Rain-wet weeds soaked his trouser legs as he walked toward them, but unexpectedly the clouds had cleared to allow weak sunlight to illuminate the sodden landscape—and the land he'd once thought of as barren was beautiful.

Ipsial caught sight of him and waved. Gerard waved back, and suddenly the pale sun suffused him with warm, vibrant light. Waves of joy washed through him, one after another, at the sight of his boy and Miles, his friend, waiting for him to join them.

Miles closed the cottage door behind Gerard and fastened the latch securely. No more interruptions. No more delay. Ipsial had been tucked safe into his bed in the abbey and had fallen asleep so fast and deeply there was little doubt he'd stay that way until morning.

After putting Ipsial to bed, Gerard had taken a stroll with Miles. They talked of the abbey's repairs, in case a servant overheard, but once they were clear of the house and in the dark shadows of night, they were free to join hands and walk together.

Despite the heavy clots of mud on his boots, Miles floated as they trod the familiar path to his cottage. He set a fire to warm the place, but it needed little heating. His flesh was already red-hot at Gerard's presence.

Miles hung up the poker and turned to face Gerard. They stood several feet apart, simply staring at each other for several long, breathless moments. Too many days had passed since their first fervent encounters. Miles felt suddenly awkward and unsure. But not for long. Gerard lunged at him, boots scraping the floor as he swooped on Miles and dragged him hard against his body.

They attacked each other with abandon, hands scrabbling to remove clothing, mouths seeking to kiss and lick every new bit of bare skin. Shirts, trousers, undergarments were discarded like wrapping paper from a gift. Gerard's late-evening stubble scraped Miles's chest as his mouth tugged painfully on one nipple, sending powerful shivers through Miles. He threaded his fingers through Gerard's hair and gripped it, relishing the silken strength of the thick strands.

Gerard straightened and curled a hand around Miles's nape, holding him hard as he kissed and kissed him. Tender nibbles of his mouth progressed into a caress with Gerard's tongue and then a wild plunging as the two attempted to devour each other whole. Miles had once been at sea during a hurricane and, minus the churning nausea of seasickness, this was rather like that. He couldn't tell up from down, and he was utterly swept away by passion.

After a few moments, Gerard broke off the kiss, leaving Miles cross-eyed and panting. He dropped to his knees, grasping Miles's hips in his hands and drawing his cock into his mouth—so hot and wet and perfectly fitting him. Miles stared at the astonishing sight of his employer on his knees, head bobbing up and down, and the visual image whipped his desire to new heights. Gerard let go of his hip to reach below and cradle his balls. He fondled them and teased a finger along the path leading to Miles's bunghole. He traced the spasming

216

entrance, then eased his finger inside.

"Aw, Christ," Miles gritted between his teeth. The sensation wasn't one he'd experienced before, and he was amazed at the desire for more than one probing finger aroused in him. He felt his rear channel opening and aching to be filled. The thought of such a thing happening, coupled with Gerard's mouth gobbling his cock, abruptly put Miles over the edge. He thrust his hips forward several times sharply and release swelled through him.

"Oh, I'm going to..." But it was too late to warn Gerard. He was already spending.

Gerard ceased the movement of his head while Miles's cock pulsed. He swallowed, then withdrew, leaving his depleted cock glistening wet.

He looked up at Miles with a twinkle in his eye. "Well, that was quick."

"I couldn't help it. I've been waiting far too long." Miles smoothed Gerard's tousled hair. "And you're far too good at that."

"Experience." Gerard stood, a smug little smirk curving his lips. "For which I'll be ever grateful. But let me assure you, I plan to practice on no man other than you for the foreseeable future, if ever." He cradled Miles's face and looked into his eyes. "It surprises me to learn that I quite literally want no one but you. I do believe this might be what the poets refer to as true love."

He spoke blithely as if making a jest, but the intensity in his eyes let Miles know Gerard meant every word. Joy and light bubbled up inside him like a pot boiling over. He could scarcely contain a desire to whoop out loud or babble his own proclamation of love. But that wasn't his way, so he said quietly, "I'm very fond of you too, sir."

Gerard laughed. "We're back to 'sir' again, are we? I think

not. During our private times together, it shall be Miles and Gerard."

"What, no Eve or Evie?" Miles teased as he snaked an arm around Gerard's back and pulled him close. Hard muscle and bone thumped together. God, how he loved the solid, unyielding feeling of Gerard's body in his arms. Made him want to wrestle the man to the ground.

"No Evie! Not ever. Don't remind me of my horrible cousin right now, or you'll wilt my desire."

"Don't think there's any danger of that." Miles ground against the erection pressing insistently into his groin. "What do you plan to do with that thing?"

Gerard leaned close and traced Miles's ear with his tongue before answering. "Close your eyes and do exactly as I say, and I'll show you."

Gerard shivered but not at the chill. He'd have Miles under him. Finally, Gerard would enter his body, possess him.

He pushed Miles to the narrow bed. The ropes groaned under their weight as he guided Miles down and then settled over him, his weight on his arms and knees, his cock against Miles's thigh.

He longed to surge into Miles, assuage the hunger, but of course he knew better. With a gusty sigh of impatience, Gerard pulled himself up and off, searching the room frantically for something that would suffice.

Miles hauled himself up on his elbows, his chest heaving. He managed to raise his eyebrows and sound coolly amused. "Changed your mind?"

"Butter." Gerard grunted the word. He sure as the devil couldn't feel amused or anything beyond his feverish need.

He fetched the earthenware bowl from the pantry and returned before Miles could sit up.

Gerard put the bowl on the floor and scooped up a handful of the butter.

"Oi," Miles began, and then, as Gerard smoothed the substance over his cock and balls, "Oh."

Miles's shaft thickened, grew hard, slippery inside Gerard's fist. Gerard slid his other hand down to the tight heat and groaned as he worked his finger into Miles's body. He released Miles to stroke butter onto his own cock, but resisted the urgent desire to tighten his hand around himself. He'd feel the squeeze of Miles around him, surrounding him.

"Don't stop." Miles arched his back, pushing up insistently.

Gerard climbed onto the bed again and knelt over him. Miles drew up his legs to allow better access, while Gerard's cock slid delightfully between his cheeks.

Gerard needed more. He held his stone-hard cock in his fist to stop himself from thrusting too hard or fast and eased into Miles's tight entrance. They both cursed as he drove in deeper and deeper still.

Too good. He pushed again but stopped when Miles moved restlessly beneath him.

"Do not stop," Miles said louder and more urgent this time.

Gerard obeyed. He pushed and felt himself go past the impossible tightness, and he was lodged deep inside his lover.

The sensation was too magnificent. Miles's small groans and hurried breaths were enough to drive him to completion.

"Hush," Gerard ordered. "Don't move."

Miles cursed and froze. Gerard rested for several heartbeats until the urgent need receded. He moved then. Slow, slow and then faster. Miles shifted under him, writhing. His full lips parted, and soon he begged incoherent phrases *please, yes.*

Then Miles reached for his own cock and pulled, whimpering with need. His head went back, his throat a graceful column, his chest heaving.

Buried balls-deep in his lover was the best possible way to witness the most erotic sight of Gerard's life. Except every motion and the tight clamping friction brought him close to his end, and his own balls begged for more.

The pleasure clutched tighter, drove him to move again. Fast and faster. He grunted as the explosion seized and rolled through him.

Under him, Miles also cried out and shuddered. His spending touched Gerard's cheek and shoulder.

Gerard pulled out and collapsed on the panting body of his lover. He kissed his cheek, his neck, tasted the salt of Miles's sweat and sperm.

He had never felt such tranquility—until Miles put his arms around him and held him closer, and he felt an even more bone-melting peace of heart and mind.

They exchanged several leisurely kisses before Miles reached for the rough blanket to cover them both. Gerard moved onto his side, pressed against Miles, their arms and legs wrapped tightly around each other.

Miles's deep laugh shook him.

"Yes?" Gerard asked.

"I'll never again butter my bread without thinking of this."

"Good." Gerard smirked. "There is the ointment I keep at the abbey. Although perhaps we might look into other methods to, ah, smooth the way."

"You want to conduct experiments?"

Gerard yawned. "Yes, a great many variations on a

delightful theme."

Miles pressed his mouth to Gerard's neck and licked him. He whispered, his breath warm on his skin, "Years of it, I pray."

Chapter Twenty-One

They waited at the station for a train that was almost an hour late. An extra hour of Ipsial's nervous questions. "What if I don't like him?"

"My nephew is an easy-going lad. He will entertain himself if you do not get along with him. And you know you're good at playing on your own."

"Playing." Ipsial's lip curled. "*I* never played."

"Then you have some catching up to do, I expect," Miles said, mild as ever. "Although you're not right about that, Ipsial. You're a fine knucklebone player. You can take him on with that game."

Ipsial brightened but only for a few seconds. "There's that girl too," he observed gloomily.

"Yes. Susan turned ten years old just last week."

"I don't know about girls."

Miles chuckled. "Mrs. Trentwell won't let you remain ignorant, and Susan will let you know how to get on."

"He's a true Gerard, that's for certain," Miles said in a low voice a few minutes and a dozen worried questions later.

"Here now," Gerard protested without heat.

By the time they spotted the dark plume of smoke in the distance, portending the train's arrival, Ipsial had fallen silent, which was almost worrisome.

"We'd thought you might want to live with them in the Rose Cottage, but if you prefer to stay at the abbey—" Gerard said.

"Yes." Ipsial nodded. "What if you like them better, though?"

"What? No. That won't happen."

The boy tugged on his crisp shirt collar, then pushed down one of his stockings to scratch his calf. He appeared ready to tear off the new clothes Miles had coerced him into, and his rumpled hair had long since lost all suggestion that it had been combed.

"They don't have a father either," he said.

"You are my son, Ipsial. That will never change, no matter how many children come to stay with us." Gerard should have been tired of saying a variation of these words. Perhaps he would grow impatient in time, but each time he repeated the sentiment, he felt as if he filled something needful in himself as well as Ipsial.

The train's whistle split the air, and they stepped back from the smoke and noise.

Mrs. Trentwell and her children were the only ones to step off the train. The two children, both shouting, ran to Miles. He caught each up in turn and squeezed them and kissed them.

Ipsial watched with narrowed eyes. He wouldn't allow affectionate gestures, but when Gerard reached down and put a hand on his shoulder, Ipsial didn't pull away. A second later, he leaned against his legs. Gerard smiled. Mrs. Trentwell's children were already teaching his son something.

Miles's sister had familiar blunt features and twinkling blue eyes in a smaller, only slightly more feminine face. She gave a shallow bob as Miles introduced her to Gerard.

"I am pleased to meet you, Mr. Gerard, Master Gerard." She solemnly shook hands with Ipsial.

Miles walked up to them with the still-noisy children

hanging on to his arms. "I'll have your things brought to the cottage, Molly." He shook his arms free and gave a mock growl of disapproval. "Goodness, these two have doubled their size since last I saw them."

"Mr. Gerard, allow me to introduce my son and daughter," Mrs. Trentwell said. "Jack and Susan, give me your attention, please." Immediately, the boy and girl stopped speaking and stood straighter. Their show of perfect manners brought on Ipsial's narrow-eyed suspicious gaze again.

Miles and Joey arranged for the Trentwell trunks to be brought to the abbey. By the time the little group moved out of the station, Ipsial strolled ahead of the adults, next to Jack Trentwell. Ipsial described Rose Cottage to an obviously impressed Jack.

"My house is bigger, of course, but you can come along any time," he said grandly.

"Oh dear," Gerard muttered. "He's going to strut about, showing off."

"Let him." Miles smiled. "Susan will let him know if he crosses any lines."

Sure enough, the little girl's piping voice reached them. "Mama says that children can't own property. It must be put in thrust or something. So it's not truly your house, is it?"

"It's my father's house. That's my father back there, with your uncle. They're together."

Oh Christ.

Gerard didn't stumble or even turn red. He glanced over at Mrs. Trentwell, who didn't appear to hear.

But Ipsial continued without pause. "They both take care of me. Now I guess your mother's helping too."

"Like having three parents?" Jack asked.

"I guess." Ipsial sounded gloomy.

Mrs. Trentwell laughed. She allowed Miles to help her into the large carriage Gerard had recently purchased. She and the children settled in.

Gerard and Miles leaped up to the driver's seat—Joey stayed behind to supervise the luggage.

"Your sister looks like you," Gerard said.

"Good heavens, never say such a thing to her. She's grateful to you, but even gratitude can only go so far. She'd hate to hear that."

"Bah. It makes me like her better."

Miles gave him one of those rare full smiles. "The fact that he looks exactly like a Gerard is one of the reasons I love young Ipsial. Shallow of me, I suppose."

"Yes," agreed Gerard.

Miles laughed and clouted him on the shoulder. "My sister will have to teach you manners as well."

"All right. And in exchange, I will teach her children to ride."

"And no doubt Ipsial will show off his skills on horseback to Jack."

Gerard groaned. "The boy still must learn to post, although he manages to hang on like a monkey."

Miles helped his sister move into the cottage while Ipsial gave her children a tour of the rest of the abbey grounds.

"I believe I shall follow behind at a discreet distance," Gerard said as the children trotted away from Rose Cottage.

He tipped his hat at Molly and Miles, then stuffed his hands into his pockets and strolled in the direction the three young ones had gone.

"He's quite different from your first description of him," Molly said as she walked around the sitting room.

"We've been civilizing him." Miles sat on the ancient horsehair sofa.

"I mean your employer, silly. He's very careful of his boy. Even if he was an ogre or as careless as you'd first described, I'd be inclined to like him."

"Yes, he's generous. And I'm glad you and the children can live somewhere decent at last."

"More than that, he is a good friend to you. You have lost your restlessness. I think you seem happy."

He and Molly were close, but some things were too much to admit even to her. "I like my position here, I like the abbey, and I'm glad to be settled near you."

"That's what I mean. You are settled and happily so."

"Yes," he said simply. "I belong here."

She picked up a jacket that had fallen from the chair where her son had abandoned it. "I know I've been brought here to help young Ipsial, but I can see he is more careful of his clothing than my Jack. They will learn from each other, I think. Thank you, Miles." She sat down next to him and grabbed his hands. "This is an ideal situation."

"I think so too." He squeezed her hands in his.

Later, Ipsial decided he'd like to try to stay the night, just one night, at Rose Cottage, just to welcome the newcomers. Miles said good night to his sister, and the three young people who were arranging the pieces of one of Jack's games called A Day at The Zoo.

He walked toward his smaller cottage and noticed that

smoke already issued from his chimney. He broke into a run, because that was a sign that Gerard waited for him.

Sure enough, Gerard sat in a chair, reading by an oil lamp.

"I think my sister suspects how important you are to me," Miles said as he hung up his coat.

Gerard put down the magazine. "Is she offended?"

"Hardly."

Gerard folded his arms, and the magazine slipped from his lap. "Then we shall be happy. I defy anyone to find a fly in the ointment."

"Don't tempt fate, Gerard." Miles grinned. "Ointment, you say? Shall I inspect the jar I know you brought down from the abbey?"

"You read my mind, Kenway."

"A good servant strives to give satisfaction even before he is asked for service." He cupped Gerard's cheek.

He enjoyed Gerard's low, delicious chuckle. But even more, he loved the way Gerard moaned under his touch and turned his head to kiss his palm.

He squatted by the chair, rested his hands on Gerard's thighs and looked him in the eye. "I am more than fond of you, Gerard."

"Ah?"

"I had never thought I would love anyone more than my family. I do. I love you."

Gerard rose from the chair and pulled him to his feet. "This is good. You are mine," he whispered as he wrapped his arms around Miles's waist.

"Oh? Possessive are you?"

"Yes. Entirely possessive when it comes to you."

Miles would have continued the flirtatious nonsense, but by then Gerard took away his words with kisses. He didn't object.

About the Authors

Summer Devon is the alter ego of Kate Rothwell who also writes under her own name. Kate/Summer lives in Connecticut. You can learn more about her books at katerothwell.com and summerdevon.com and facebook.com/S.DevonAuthor.

To learn more about Bonnie Dee go to bonniedee.com. Send an email to Bonnie Dee at bondav40@yahoo.com. Join her Yahoo! group at http://groups.yahoo.com/group/bonniedee. Her Facebook address is facebook.com/bonnie.dee.144 or you can follow her on Twitter: @Bonnie_Dee.

Trusting a psychic flash might solve a mystery...and lead to love.

The Psychic and the Sleuth
© *2011 Bonnie Dee and Summer Devon*

Inspector Robert Court should have felt a sense of justice when a rag-and-bones man went to the gallows for murdering his cousin. Yet something has never felt right about the investigation. Robert's relentless quest for the truth has annoyed his superintendent, landing him lowly assignments such as foiling a false medium who's fleecing the wives of the elite.

Oliver Marsh plays the confidence game of spiritualism, though his flashes of insight often offer his clients some comfort. Despite the presence of an attractive, if sneering, non-believer at a séance, he carries on—and experiences a horrifying psychic episode in which he experiences a murder *as the victim.*

There's only one way for Court to learn if the young, dangerously attractive Marsh is his cousin's killer or a real psychic: spend as much time with him as possible. Despite his resolve to focus on his job, Marsh somehow manages to weave a seductive spell around the inspector's straight-laced heart.

Gradually, undeniable attraction overcomes caution. The two men are on the case, and on each other, as they race to stop a murderer before he kills again.

Warning: Graphic language and hot male/male sex with light BDSM themes. Despite "Descriptions of Murderous Acts" perpetrated by an unhinged killer, resist the temptation to cover your eyes—you'll miss the good parts!

Available now in ebook and print from Samhain Publishing.

His deadliest enemy will become his heart's desire.

Brothers of the Wild North Sea
© *2013 Harper Fox*

Caius doesn't feel like much of a Christian. He loves his life of learning as a monk in the far-flung stronghold of Fara, but the hot warrior blood of his chieftain father flows in his veins. Heat soothed only in the arms of his sweet-natured friend and lover, Leof.

When Leof is killed during a Viking raid, Cai's grieving heart thirsts for vengeance—and he has his chance with Fenrir, a wounded young Viking warrior left for dead. But instead of reaching for a weapon, Cai finds himself defying his abbot's orders and using his healing skills to save Fen's life.

At first, Fen repays Cai's kindness by attacking every Christian within reach. But as time passes, Cai's persistent goodness touches his heart. And Cai, who had thought he would never love again, feels the stirring of a profound new attraction.

Yet old loyalties call Fen back to his tribe and a relentless quest to find the ancient secret of Fara—a powerful talisman that could render the Vikings indestructible, and tear the two lovers' bonds beyond healing.

Warning: Contains battles, bloodshed, explicit M/M sex, and the proper Latin term for what lies beneath those cassocks.

Available now in ebook and print from Samhain Publishing.

It's all about the story...

Romance

HORROR

www.samhainpublishing.com

CPSIA information can be obtained at www.ICGtesting.com
Printed in the USA
LVOW06s2233050814

397735LV00004B/249/P